USA TODAY BESTSELLING AUTHOR
Dale Mayer

Jace's JEWEL

HEROES FOR HIRE

JACE'S JEWEL: HEROES FOR HIRE, BOOK 12
Beverly Dale Mayer
Valley Publishing Ltd.

ISBN-13: 978-1-773360-57-7
Print Edition

Books in This Series:

Carson's Choice: Heroes for Hire, Book 28
Dante's Decision: Heroes for Hire, Book 29
Steven's Solace: Heroes for Hire, Book 30

Boxed Sets and Bundles
https://geni.us/Bundlepage

About This Book

When several members of a search and rescue team die in an accident, followed by several more team members who are murdered, Jace is ordered to sort it out.

Working for a large insurance company had always been great for Emily, until she is handed several files all from the same family. Men she knew… intimately. Afraid there is too much going on in the background she contacts Legendary Securities for help.

As the investigation develops, more bodies turn up, along with jealousy, greed and insurance payouts that just maybe shouldn't have been paid.

She pairs up with the sexy Jace as they delve into the twisted and personal cases and race to stop another murder from taking place right in front of them…

Sign up to be notified of all Dale's releases here!
https://geni.us/DaleNews

Chapter 1

J ACE COLLEY SAT at the end of the long dining room table at the compound. It had taken him one week to adjust to being part of a large group again. He had regained that sense of brotherhood he'd had in the military. That sense of belonging to a bigger cause. When Michael, a good friend and teammate from his old unit, had called and told Jace about Levi, Jace had jumped at the chance. As had Tyson. Jace had done a few jobs for Levi, and each one confirmed Jace had made the right decision. Rory was dragging his feet, as were Liam and Brandon. But they'd come around eventually.

Jace couldn't believe how many lived and worked here. Levi had invested heavily in living accommodations.

The first of the couples were moving into the finished apartments this coming weekend. Levi had rehabbed one of the buildings to accommodate his men. It was a great idea. And it certainly ensured people would remain with the company. Not that it was an issue as far as Jace could see. Loyalty shone from the men's faces.

Levi walked in, talking on his phone. "Terkel, I'm putting you on the monitor."

He reached for the remote below a large screen on the dining room wall as a man appeared in front of them. Jace studied the face and gave a slow smile. "What the hell,

Terkel?"

Terkel had been quiet, his gaze roaming the faces in front of him. When he saw Jace, his face cracked into a big smile. "Jace, what the hell, man. You found your way here, like a homing pigeon. Damn, you're looking good."

"Well, I got out before I ended up in pieces," Jace said with a smile. "What the hell are you doing with this lot?"

"I'm always around," Terkel said. "You never know when or where I'll pop up. Besides Merk's been part of this company since the beginning. I have to keep an eye out for my brother."

"Good thing, considering it's a third eye," Merk said with a grin. He leaned back in his seat, raising the front legs off the floor. "What's with the haircut?"

Terkel shook his head. Long dark-brown curls shifted in waves. "I'm heading undercover."

Merk sat forward, his chair legs coming down hard. "What the hell?"

Terkel's face hardened. "Don't even try to talk me out of it. I can't explain, as you well know. But I could be a free agent at the end of this," he joked. "If you're looking for new hires, I might be in a position to apply."

Levi's voice was quiet but clear. "I always have room for you here, Terkel, but I know you. You'd want to have your own supersecret spy agency, working black ops missions off the books."

"Something that couldn't happen of course," Terkel said. "On the other hand, the brass is bubbling in my ear about a similar topic."

Merk shook his head. "I don't like the sound of this."

"It doesn't matter if you do or not, bro." Terkel's face cracked into a smile. "I'll be fine. Besides, that's not why I'm calling."

Levi snorted. "Of course not. What do you know?"

"This is not through my military channels but through my underground network. TxSAR, the Austin Texas Search and Rescue team, was called in to help when Austin's Blanco River flooded its banks. A bridge went down there on the rivers that feed into it. In the process, two of the TxSAR men were swept away in the floodwaters. Another two members died, not while on duty, but definitely due to foul play."

Jace studied Terkel's face. "What happened to them?"

"One death looks like a hit-and-run."

Several of the women at the table winced.

Jace narrowed his gaze. "But?"

"He was already dead. It was made to look like the vehicle ran over him accidentally. Water is involved in the fourth case, but ..."

Levi leaned forward. "And why do you think any of it ties in?"

Terkel gave an approving nod. "All I can tell you is they do. But what I can't tell you is how. That's for you guys to figure out."

Ice snorted. "Terkel, I love your sixth sense, or whatever you want to call it, but I need a little more than that to justify a team looking into these deaths."

His gaze shifted to Ice, and his face lit up. "Damn, you get better looking every time I see you."

"Time to get yourself a partner, Terkel," Levi said jokingly.

He shook his head. "Not yet. Timing is not quite right. But soon."

"If anyone of us had listened to that same line, none of us would've ended up with the partners we have," Merk said.

"I'd love to see you settled down, bro."

"It's coming." Terkel got a far-off look in his eye. "And faster than I had expected," he admitted. "But it won't be easy, and it won't be sweet. She's in trouble but doesn't know it."

The room went silent.

"Who?" Ice asked. "Who's in trouble?"

"I have no idea." Terkel laughed. "Welcome to my world. However, that's not today's issue. She doesn't show up for a few more months. And you guys will all be instrumental with helping her." Terkel's gaze sharpened. "Right now we have four TxSAR men dead, and I highly suspect there could be more – or if not stopped – will be more. Not all were in paid positions. Several were volunteers."

"I still need a reason or something that links them together to make it worthy of a full-scale investigation," Ice said patiently. "And the TxSAR units have their own ways of investigating issues like this. They will bring in the police if need be."

He nodded. "All I can tell you is, they are from the same family."

Jace straightened. "They're all brothers?"

"They're all cousins. And I'll give you the heads-up. The TxSAR organization will call you any moment."

Ice shook her head. "Not likely. Again they have their own protocol in place within their system."

Terkel gave her a ghost of a smile. "Oh, Ice. You have so little faith." And just like that, he hung up, and the screen went black.

Ice turned toward Merk. "He gets a little weirder every day."

Merk chuckled. "He does indeed. But, as we well know,

he's special."

Jace said, "Four cousins?"

Levi nodded. "Chances are he's right."

Merk and Levi exchanged looks.

"He usually is," Merk said.

"But it still doesn't mean we have any right to step in."

The phone rang in Levi's hand. He checked it, looked at Ice, then said, "Do you want to talk to TxSAR, or do I?"

She glared at him, snatched the phone from his hand, and introduced herself. "How can I help you?" She put it on Speakerphone.

"This is Conway Dunlap of TxSAR. I have a delicate situation here, and we could use some help."

She smothered a laugh but took the phone off Speaker and left the room.

Under his breath Jace whispered, "Damn. I forgot how on the mark Terkel so often is."

Merk, at his side, leaned over. "You have no idea."

Over the compound's loudspeaker boomed Stone's voice. "Incoming."

Jace knew it would take a while to get used to that. To him, *incoming* still meant *enemy attack*. Here it meant *company*. But they didn't get a ton of that for Stone to announce.

"A lone female, late twenties, driving a Mercedes," Stone continued. "And her marital status is single, based on a quick run of her plates and a glance at her social data. Better make sure Jace is around. He's the only single male left among us."

"I'd like to stay that way too," Jace said. "So now that we know she's likely pretty and wealthy, do we make other guesstimates before she gets here?"

Merk laughed. "It'll be connected to TxSAR."

"Terk has been a busy boy lately," Jace said.

Logan walked in then from the garage. "My father is nothing if not busy too. He just called. He's sending someone our way but wouldn't go into details. This could be them arriving now."

Levi told him about Terkel's phone call.

"Interesting." Logan walked over to the front door and stepped out, leaving the door open.

Jace could hear voices, but he raised an eyebrow at the sound of the deep female voice. Smoky and sexy, it hit his libido with a hard bang. And that brought more of the same to mind.

He watched as a tall willowy brunette walked in. Dressed in slacks and a light sleeveless top of sky blue, her stride said she had a purpose.

Logan said, "This is Emily. Dad sent her."

Emily spoke up. "I'm Emily Leacock. I work for America Plus Life Insurance. I live and work in Austin. Gunner Redding suggested I contact your group." She frowned as she stared at the sea of faces in front of her. "I'm looking for Levi."

Levi raised a hand. "I'm Levi. Ice will be here in a few moments." He motioned at the empty chairs in front of her. "Take a seat."

"Does this have to do with the four dead TxSAR members?" Jace asked.

Emily looked startled, but she quickly sat down. "I hadn't heard there were four. I was looking into the death of the first two. We carried life insurance policies on both of them ..."

"But?" Jace asked when she hesitated as if she wanted to say more. "Is there a reason not to pay out?"

She gave him a ghost of a smile. "That's the question. I was closing the files when the third man died. And that's when I became very suspicious. After checking further, I found the third man had the same amount of life insurance."

"Of course it's way too simplistic to consider that all three have the same beneficiary."

She gave a clipped nod. "Exactly. They are all different."

Levi leaned forward. "How can we help?"

"I need to know if they're related, if these men were murdered. Or if they were suicides."

"Does it make a difference to the payout one way or the other?" Levi asked.

"It depends on who ends up receiving the money at the end of the day. If they were accidental or murdered by another party, then the payouts are not an issue. If any of the beneficiaries have a hand in a person's death, then, yes, it makes a huge difference. However, if it was suicide, then there is no payout. Hence the great lengths some people go to hide their actions so their loved ones receive the insurance monies."

Jace leaned forward, studying her face. "What else?"

She looked startled for a moment but recovered quickly. With a glance around at the sea of faces, she locked onto Jace's and asked, "Why does there have to be something else?"

"Because of the fear I see in the back of your eyes. Something deeply unsettles you about this."

"Murder is an unsettling business."

Jace narrowed his gaze. "You're hedging."

She gave him a flat stare, definitely trying to put him in his place and shut him up, but that wasn't happening.

He leaned back to open his body language and stop her

from feeling quite so threatened. "Did you know the men?"

She took a deep breath and nodded. "Yes, and you're right. That's a huge issue for me."

"How well did you know them?" Merk asked.

She turned her gaze on him, but still Jace could see the whisper of pain cross her face as she said, "Very well."

"All of them?" Jace asked incredulously. Again that stare of hers was turned in his direction, and he realized how his comment had come across. Still, to think she had an affair or a relationship with four cousins was a bit much. Or was it?

"I was married to the first victim," she said. "Straight out of high school. We were divorced one year later. In the small community we were from, divorce was frowned upon. I headed for college. He went off and did his own thing. In college I had a relationship with the second victim. I didn't know he was related to my ex-husband as they hadn't lived in the same town at the time I was there. That relationship lasted about six months. A couple years later the third victim and I met at a party. He introduced himself as my ex-husband's cousin. We were engaged until I found him in bed with another woman." She shrugged. "I didn't know anything about a fourth murder until I got here. So I'm really hoping it's not somebody I know."

"I don't have any names yet," Levi stated. "But you're extremely involved. Possibly in the center of it all."

She nodded. "It's quite possible that I am," she confessed. "And that's terrifying. And that's why I need someone independent to investigate these cases. I can't appear to be biased in any way."

Silence descended on the group.

"A large insurance settlement is involved in each case. This needs to be resolved. If nothing criminal is involved, that's perfect. I'll close all these files and write checks so people can get on with their lives and try to deal with the loss of a loved one. However, if something else is going on …"

Jace heard the pain threading through her coming out in her voice and thought about the position she was in.

She settled back. "I'm hoping you can help me."

"You shouldn't be handling the cases at all," Jace said bluntly. "Not if you know these men personally."

She nodded. "Normally I wouldn't, but we're crammed with claims right now from the two recent hurricanes, and we're terribly short-staffed. So my boss is overseeing my work on this one. And, yes, he knows about my personal relationships with each."

Ice studied her for a long time.

Jace knew both Levi and Ice would decide, but, when it came to assessing people—particularly women—well, that was all Ice's specialty.

Ice said, "We need more information. And why did Gunner send you to us?"

"He said you can make discreet inquiries and get to the bottom of this fast," Emily said bluntly. "I'm hoping he's right."

"TxSAR has already asked us to look into it," Ice said. "Naturally we would've uncovered your relationship with the three men, so it's good you're here."

"My company is also prepared to hire you. We need to know what happened."

Ice stood. "Come to my office." She picked up her cup, realized Emily didn't have one, motioned to the pot, and said, "Bring a cup with you if you want."

Emily nodded gratefully. She stood, walked over to pour a cup of coffee, then turned to Ice, cup in hand. "Lead on."

The two women disappeared from the room. Jace sat there for a long moment, then said, "Anybody else think that's weird?"

"It's weird, but it's not that weird," Merk said. "Most people have relationships with those they know. And that usually means the extended family of those they know. That's how people meet. You go to a family gathering or a party and meet somebody. You have a relationship with them, but, in the process, you meet their extended family and friends, so the circle of who you know widens. Within that group you meet someone else. But she's been in a relationship with three who have died with possibly large insurance payouts. *That* is weird. And puts her right in the middle of it all. But what we need to do is get the names of the latest deceased and find out if she knows the fourth man."

"It's a good thing she's the one writing the checks, not the one cashing them." Jace snorted. "She'd be at the top of our list."

When Levi's phone rang, he got up and left the room to answer it.

Jace watched him leave, but his mind was spinning with all they didn't know. "We also need to find out if any other men from the same family are in the TxSAR ranks. And do any of them have a large life insurance policy? While we sort out the victims, we have to make sure there aren't any more potential targets."

EMILY TOOK A seat in Ice's office, a large space with six desks in the room and still vacant space for more.

"This is quite the operation you have here," she said.

"It's coming along nicely," Ice responded. "I'm sorry you're in this mess. It appears you're in the center of it all."

"And that's not where I want to be," Emily said, her voice thin, wan. "Who would?"

"True enough." They fell into a discussion of what Emily's company needed from Legendary Security. Finally done, Ice turned her light-blue gaze on Emily. "Before you leave, is there anything else you need to tell us?"

Startled, Emily looked at her. "What do you mean?"

"Through this investigation we will get into everybody's lives. And although I'm sure you telling us about the three men wasn't the easiest, if there's more, things you don't want to tell us, we will find out. So it's much easier to tell me now."

Emily winced. "It's not even bad." She groaned, then studied Ice. "It's just, growing up, I went through many different stages. This is my natural hair color now. When I was younger, I hated who I was, so I was always changing, trying to be someone else. Each of the men knew me as somebody else." She shrugged. "I don't even think it's important that you know that. But it's something I didn't do particularly well. So, when you hear about their wives, girlfriends, know that one was a redhead, one had black hair, and one was blonde, but they were all me."

Ice nodded, pulled out her notepad and jotted this down.

Emily found this painful, going through the names of the men she'd been with.

"The other thing is they all have different surnames. They don't look alike. They don't act alike. You wouldn't know they were related."

"And no need to feel bad even if you could tell they were

related," Ice said firmly. "We're not in the Victorian times where you're not allowed to have relationships out of wedlock."

Emily laughed. "A darn good thing. Otherwise I would be in jail or worse."

"So would most of us. Now let's get to the men, one at a time. Can you remember what hair color you were using with each?"

"In high school I was a redhead. That was with Ronnie."

"Ronnie?"

Emily pulled a notebook from her purse. "I made notes myself to figure out what the hell was going on at each time." She flipped to the right page. "Ronnie Williamson was my high school sweetheart. We married one week after graduation. Split one year later."

Ice nodded. "Next?"

Emily went to the next page. "That was Howard. His last name was Waterton. We only dated for about six months. I went with black hair at the time. Very short, cropped, like a pixie cut."

Ice smiled and kept writing.

"The third man was Lyle Cowichan. And I was a blonde then."

Ice laughed. "Did you find it made any difference?"

"Not one bit," Emily said. "I still couldn't change what was on the inside."

Ice studied her. "Why would you want to?"

Emily winced. "I've always blamed myself for my little brother's death in a house fire when we were growing up. I hated myself. So I spent decades trying to change into someone other than the person I saw in the mirror. The horrible big sister who couldn't save her baby brother," she said quietly. "I went through a number of shrinks and relationships where I tried to outrun my past. Finally I came to terms with the fact that I was only ten, and I probably wasn't capable of doing very much more than I did, which was to get myself out."

Sympathy filled Ice's gaze. "The trials of childhood. They seem to follow us right into adulthood, no matter what we do."

"In my case it didn't help that my parents blamed me. They reminded me of it day in and day out for the rest of my growing years. Until my father drank himself to death, and my mother remarried. But I was part of her painful past, so let's just say that I don't see her at all." Emily shook her head. "Why am I telling you this? I guess maybe it will help you understand why I need to know what's going on with these cases. To make sure that three men I cared for, however briefly, who are now dead, have not died because of me."

"Understood. I need your full name and the contact information for these men if you have it and how they're related."

"Their family tree is a little complicated. They are first cousins. Six daughters with eighteen children between them. All married so have different surnames. Several family members have since died."

"Right. So I'll draw a family tree. Do you have that information on you?"

Emily picked up her briefcase to pull out her file. "This is what I pulled together from the records." She held out a copy. "You can keep it."

Ice picked it up, took a look, and nodded. "This is helpful." She turned toward Emily. "And how much are the payouts?"

"One million each for the three men."

Ice nodded. "Do you know if any other family members are in TxSAR? And do you know if any other family members have life insurance policies?"

"I don't," Emily said. "I don't have access to answer your first question. And we have hundreds of thousands of policies to sort through, with different surnames in the mix. I'll look into it when I return to the office."

"And how many children did the eighteen children have?"

"Twenty-two." Emily laughed as Ice winced. "Exactly. And I don't have all those names either. I'm trying to build that level of the tree. Then I'll see if we hold policies on anyone else in the extended family."

Levi walked in then. Emily turned and smiled at him. He leaned against one of the desks close to them. "Do you know a Richard Manton?"

Emily looked at him and frowned. "I'm not sure. I know several Richards."

Levi gave a nod. "Maybe that's a good thing.

"Why's that?"

"He's the fourth victim. The one they know was definitely murdered."

Inside she could feel relief blossoming through her. That meant these men weren't targeted because of her. "I'd have to see a photo of him to be sure, but the name isn't ringing any bells."

"I'm bringing up a photo now." He tapped the tablet in his hand.

"This is what I have." Ice turned the laptop her way. "Do you know this man?"

Emily looked at it and gasped. "Oh, my God! I do." She sank back in the chair, a look of horror on her face. "He's dead?"

"Yes. How do you know him?" Ice asked.

She shook her head. "Because Lyle had to get a restraining order against him for his wife."

"Lyle, your ex-fiancé, the third dead man?"

"Yes. His wife was the girlfriend I found him in bed with. But apparently her ex-boyfriend wasn't done with her yet. That's him."

"So you're involved but not on a personal level this time. Good," Ice stated. "How did you hear about the restraining order?"

"Friends in common. He was pointed out at a restaurant we were at one evening." Bewildered she added, "I'm not sure what you mean by that first part, but, if you're asking if I ever slept with Richard, the answer is no."

Levi nodded. "Good enough. Make sure we have a way to contact you at all times. Everyone and anyone could be involved. We don't know exactly what's going on yet," he said with a sharp look at her. "Stay safe."

A little shaky she rose, shook hands with both of them, and followed Ice to the kitchen, Emily's mind washed in pain. She understood Levi's need to warn her, but it never occurred to her that this killer could be a threat to her. She didn't love easy. To know three of the dead men were people she had cared about—two deeply—was a blow she struggled with. Knowing the fourth man was someone she knew also, well …

In the dining room again, she mustered up a smile for those gathered at the table. She didn't quite understand how, or even if, they all belonged to this place, but she'd heard from Gunner that they were a large team.

As she walked toward the front door, one of the men hopped up, walked over, and held it open for her. In a low voice he asked, "Are you okay?"

"I'm not sure," she admitted. "Levi said I needed to make sure I stayed safe. There could be a connection, and the killer could be coming after me."

"I'm sure he was saying that more as a warning. You're not in TxSAR, and you're not a part of the same family."

She took a deep breath, nodded, and smiled. "Thank you for that."

He held up his hand. "I'm Jace. If you need to get a hold of anybody here, you can contact any of us. We'll be happy to help."

She smiled. "Thank you." She walked on alone to her vehicle.

He still stood there when she reversed out of the lot and headed to the main road. Once again she wondered at the wisdom of doing what she'd done. Should she have contacted them? Or had she opened herself up for a whole lot more pain?

Chapter 2

B Y THE TIME Emily returned to her office, her boss, Wilson, waited for her. "Where were you?"

"Out in the field," she said. "I spoke to Gunner about Legendary Security, then drove down to see them myself."

"Do you think they're reputable?" Wilson asked nervously.

She smiled. Dimpled and pudgy—everywhere—Wilson was one of the nicest men she knew. That he was blissfully married to an equally pear-shaped woman and had five children made Emily love him that much more. But when it came to the job and the company, he was a worrywart. And she was sure a heart attack awaited him somewhere in the next few years.

"They're very reputable. We're right to do this. It's also won't cost us much at all because TxSAR has already brought them in."

At that Wilson's eyebrows popped right up. "So they are also wondering if these deaths were suspicious?"

"I'm sure they are," she said simply. "I'm equally sure TxSAR is covering their asses in case lawsuits come in."

Wilson rolled his eyes at that. "What would we do without all the lovely lawsuits to keep the judicial system flowing?" he muttered and walked back into his small office. "We have a lot of other cases so don't spend too much time on those," he warned. "The head office is chewing on my butt again."

She chuckled to herself. She wanted to say, *Lots to chew on*, but that was mean, and she wasn't mean-hearted. But he made that comment probably once a day. And by now it had lost its bite.

Back in her cubicle, she sat to update her notes on the cases. She opened her own file and added the information on the fourth victim. Part of her job did require running down all kinds of information on people, and she was amazed at how much fraud existed in insurance claims.

The things people did to each other over money. She understood the appeal of having lots of money, but she'd much prefer to have friends and family rather than kill them off. Plus she earned her money the old-fashioned way, by working hard.

As she returned to her email, she found her in-box full, plus the physical folders on several pending investigations were stacked high on the side of her desk. She groaned at the sight. The topmost folder was an especially volatile subject. An elderly woman who'd been paying faithfully on a life insurance policy had now passed away. Her daughter was the beneficiary, and the grandchildren declared the daughter incompetent—just to get their hands on the life insurance proceeds. Emily had emails from lawyers on both sides of the issue. Technically it had nothing to do with her. The paperwork was legal and binding. The daughter was the beneficiary. That's all there was to it. Only it was never that simple. Not with everyone trying to work the system to their advantage. The one grandson in particular was being very vocal about the mental state of his mother and why she shouldn't get the money. Still it wasn't Emily's problem.

Legal precedents had to be followed. But these kinds of issues kept crossing her desk and chewing up her time, which ate into her productivity.

By the time she closed the last folder, doing as much as she could on several different cases, the back of her neck was tight, and her forehead pounded with the start of a headache. She stood and realized the office was already empty. In fact, it looked like everybody was gone.

With a frown she checked her watch. She was a good forty minutes past her normal quitting time. "Crap."

She'd take the time off another day because Wilson hated it when she claimed overtime. He was of the opinion that everyone should get their work done by closing time. The trouble was, in this job, the work was never done as she always had more open case files than she could possibly close. Right now she didn't have any checks to write because she had no cases cleared. And she'd been doing this work for the company for four years. She found it fascinating and depressing at the same time. She loved writing checks she knew would make a difference in people's lives. But it always came at a cost. In order for them to get the money, somebody had to die.

It always revived her love of humanity when the beneficiaries were devastated at the loss of their parent or child, enough that they hesitated taking the check. But too often it was the opposite. People would jump at the check and laugh all the way to the bank, making all kinds of heartless comments, like, "The old geezer gave me something." "Bitch finally got hers." "If I'd known that old miser had that kind of money, I'd have knocked her off decades ago."

Emily wanted to go home and cleanse herself in the shower.

As she walked past Wilson's office, the lights were off, and the door was closed. She frowned. It was unlike him to leave without saying goodbye. He was extremely conscientious normally. Always did a final check to make sure everybody was gone. Based on that habit he could still be here.

She pulled out her phone and called him. "Wilson, where are you?"

"I'm leaving the office now," he said. "Where are you?"

"By the front door. Is anybody else here?"

He laughed. "Turn and you will see me."

She spun around, her phone at her ear, and saw him behind her with his big smile. She hung up her phone and tucked it into her pocket. "I didn't see you before."

Making a gesture, he smiled and motioned at her. "I was in the washroom. We can leave together."

Outside they walked to the parking lot. "Are you nervous in the office alone?" he asked, a frown forming.

She shook her head. "No, I was just surprised."

"That's good. Have a good night."

She got into her vehicle and waved at him. Then she pulled out of her space. Wilson was a caring man. He loved to go home to his family. She was heading home to an empty apartment, feeling down. Especially knowing three of the men she'd had relationships with had all passed away—and probably not naturally.

The trip to Legendary Security had given her a lot to think about.

She didn't realize how bad their deaths were until she got home and looked into the details a little more. Particularly when she found out about the fourth man. She didn't know him personally, but she definitely had a connection to him. With the initial three deaths, she'd lost an ex-husband, an ex-boyfriend, and an ex-fiancé. Did one have anything to do with the other? It was too much of a coincidence that they were from the same family and in TxSAR and connected to her. Yet it didn't make any sense.

She hated ugly cases. She'd had a few. A mother who killed her son for the insurance money. Thankfully she'd been caught. But that wouldn't bring back the little boy.

At home, she put on the teakettle, then got changed. She needed to look for the police reports from the deaths. The media had covered the two drownings because the men had been rescuing others. That made it worse. It was one thing dying by accident. That happened. It wasn't good, but nobody was to blame. To consider this might be a criminal investigation …

As she made a simple salad, she went over her list of things to do. She needed to get an update from Ice. Or if she wasn't available, she could call Jace. On the other hand, if they had found something, they'd contact her.

Her phone rang, and she glanced at the number before answering it.

"This is Jace. We met at Levi's compound today."

She smiled. "Yes. Do you have any news?" She continued on, not giving him the chance to answer. "I wanted to call when I got home, but I figured it was too soon."

"No, we don't have anything new. But we need more information from you."

"From me?"

"Yes. We need the names of the beneficiaries listed on the policies."

She groaned. "I don't have that information with me, but I can log on to the office server and get it." She opened her laptop and turned it on. "Give me a few minutes. I'm booting it up now."

"I can give you that much," he said with laughter in his voice. "Did you just get home?"

She nodded and realized he couldn't see her. "Yes. I stayed late at the office."

"I guess your job is always busy."

"Really busy. There doesn't seem to be any shortage of deaths and disasters in the world."

"You're preaching to the choir. We deal with all that every day."

"Will someone talk to the TxSAR members?"

"I'm leaving early tomorrow," he said. "That's the reason I want this information. I'll visit each site where the men died. I'll be in Austin for several days."

"You're not coming alone, right?" she asked sharply.

A few moments of silence passed by before he answered. "Are you worried about me?" There was more than passing curiosity in his tone.

She groaned. "I seem to be edgy right now. Maybe because four men in my past have died. And I realize you probably know how to take care of yourself, but I wouldn't say any of these men were a slouch in that department either."

"Tell me about them."

"Ronnie and Howard were very active volunteers. Always out helping people during natural disasters. Exactly where they'd excel. They had a multitude of survival skills. What they probably didn't have was a whole lot of martial arts skills. They lived for helping others. TxSAR was a perfect outlet for them." She reached up and rubbed her temple. "I don't know what their full TxSAR training might have entailed."

"I will find that out," Jace said. "Were they also fisher-men? Would they have known this area by the river?"

She gave him the little bit of information she knew. "Ronnie was a local guy, knew those rivers. Definitely family-oriented. He wanted to get married right out of high school. That was his wish, not mine, but I was a lovestruck teenager, and this was my *forever* love," she said in a whimsi-cal note. "As it lasted all of a year, we know that didn't work out so well."

"Was he ever abusive? Did he make enemies easily? Any-one he hated?"

"Back then he was the most popular kid on the block. He was good at sports and the teacher's pet. If ever some-body was most likely to succeed, it was him. At the same time, because of that, he might've made enemies. But I don't know of any. Even now, as I realize he's dead, my heart is filled with sorrow. He was a good man and will be missed."

"Did he marry again?"

"Yes. He was married, I believe. But I don't know any-thing about it. I don't know if he has any children or what his relationship might've been with his cousins. I suppose that's important too."

"Yes, it is. When you knew him, was there any fighting within the family?"

"Not that I know of, but can you honestly say you've met any family with no disputes, pitting one against the other?" she asked.

AT THE CRACK of dawn the next morning, Jace sat at the kitchen table, hugging his cup of coffee, a notepad in front of him. He'd been working in the office, but it was noisy up there, so he'd come downstairs to make some calls.

Logan walked in and sat beside him. "Did I hear you talking to that sexy voice again?"

Jace turned to look at him. "If you mean Emily, then, yes."

"That one could make a killing on a sex phone line," he joked.

Jace smiled. "I have to admit that I had the same thought when she was here yesterday."

The two men exchanged looks of humor.

"We never did hear how she knew Gunner."

"I just got off the phone with him," Logan said. "He's dealt with her for the last four years, since she began at America Plus Life Insurance. With my father's many business interests, he deals with a lot of insurance issues."

"That makes sense."

Logan chuckled. "While it makes sense, he also did some digging. She's single, even after the multitude of cousins she's apparently been involved with, and he's never heard anything even slightly bad against her. She is respected in the industry, and she's always been pleasant to him."

"That's good to know." Jace turned his coffee cup around in his hand several times, remembering Emily's voice.

"So she's single and available."

That's when Jace realized where Logan was going with this. Jace snorted. "What's this? Matchmaking?"

"Hell, yes. In case you haven't noticed, you're the only single guy left here."

At that he rolled his eyes. "But I wasn't when I came. Tyson wasn't hooked up then."

"But Tyson is now, very firmly attached at the hip to his

ladylove. And that leaves you off in the wind by yourself. Even Michael has Mercy."

Jace shrugged. "Emily is a client. That's hardly conducive to a relationship. Maybe after Austin, when this is all over, I could look her up."

"Sure, that might work. You ready to go?" He pointed at Jace's coffee. "We can take travel cups if you need more."

Jace stood. "I'm good. I heard somebody else was coming with me but hadn't heard who."

"Decision made. I'd rather be on the job anyway." Logan grinned. "I prefer to be busy."

"What about Flynn? Isn't he due back today?"

Logan shook his head. "He's been delayed another day. The flights are all completely grounded in Boston."

"It happens."

"The weather's been pretty crappy all summer. Flynn and Tyson weren't expecting to be in Boston. But the plane was redirected, so that's where they sit right now."

Jace walked over, grabbed his jacket off the hook on the wall, and turned to Logan. "Are you driving, or am I?"

"Do you know the area?" Logan asked.

Jace shook his head. "No."

"Then you're driving. The best way to learn the area is to drive it."

That surprised Jace. But he appreciated it. Too often he ended up slotted as an observer because he was the newcomer. Although not the only one soon. Levi had another group of men coming in. But, for the moment, Jace was still at the bottom of the totem pole. Besides, he would rather drive than be a passenger any day. He grabbed the keys. "Do we need any tools or equipment on this job?"

Logan stopped, considered the matter for a moment,

and said, "I wouldn't expect so. We're looking at the location of the four deaths. Outside of laptops and maybe decent hiking boots for walking rough terrain we should be fine."

"How long ago did the first two die?"

"Two weeks."

They headed to the truck and hopped in. Jace started the engine and pulled out of the compound. "Was it only four days later after the drownings that the third and fourth men died?"

Logan took out his notebook, flipped through to check something, and said, "Yes. Looks like it. June 27 and July 1. The first two are similar, the third and fourth are not. All possibilities must be considered."

Jace took a turn onto the main highway, heading north. "If you know a better way to get there, let me know."

"I'll give you directions when we get closer. Stay on this road for the next half hour." Logan slouched in his seat, stretching out his legs. "Did anybody get more details about TxSAR?"

"Ice is on it. This group is all volunteers who go through intensive training. So they should've been prepared for anything. Of course Mother Nature takes every opportunity to remind us who is boss. Between the floodwaters racing along, the storm was pounding them with rain from above, so they were slammed with water coming from all directions." Jace stretched out his hands one at a time. They were stiff this morning.

"Right. If the water rose very quickly, and they had no place to go, vehicles would shift in a flood. So the volunteers could've been pinned, or they could've been knocked unconscious."

"We did get the autopsies," Jace said. "Both men had

water in their lungs, their bodies banged up in a way that was consistent with being caught in the raging river. Once swept away in their vehicle, they would have struggled to get out of the vehicle and would have gotten banged up in the process. If they had taken a hit to the head somewhere along the line, they'd have gone under quickly."

"Do we have the autopsies on the other two?" Logan asked.

"No, not yet," Jace said. "Different hospital, different detectives involved. Getting those autopsy reports might take a little longer. According to Ice, Detective Dickerson is coordinating the cases in Austin, so we should meet him to get a copy of the reports ourselves." He glanced at Logan. "I'd like to know as much as we can about any wives of the deceased too."

"Of the four, only two seem to be married, Ronnie and Lyle. I don't have Ronnie's marital info yet, but I do on Lyle. I have her name and info from my phone call earlier. Sicily Ranger married Lyle Cowichan six months ago. They were apparently very happy. Her ex-boyfriend was a problem before she got married. He continued to be a problem after she was married. But nobody saw this coming."

"No, but it's not hard to imagine. We see this kind of behavior escalation a lot."

"What did you find out about what the wife said to the authorities?" Logan asked.

"According to her statement to the police, they were having a barbecue in their backyard with a few friends. Her ex-boyfriend showed up. Her husband and ex got into an altercation." He checked his notes. "The guests sent Richard packing, and Lyle went inside to calm down. When he didn't return, Sicily went looking for him. Found no sign of him. The guests all joined in the search, and he was found on the street where he'd been run over. The police went in search of Richard but couldn't locate him. Several hours later a call came in to the station that Richard was found dead in his vehicle across from where Lyle's body was found."

"I don't suppose Detective Mannford is on this case, is he?"

"No, wrong city. But, if we need any extra information, I'm sure he won't mind getting it for us."

"If he can. The last two men were TxSAR members as well, correct?" Jace asked.

"Correct."

"The first two look like accidents, could have been accidents. The second two look like a fight gone from bad to worse, definitely murder."

They arrived at the river less than three hours later. "Do we know where they went in the river?"

"Almost one mile upriver from here. The TxSAR teams, along with several passersby, were trying to rescue victims trapped inside four vehicles that fell off the bridge into the water. Nobody knows exactly what happened, but, when they did a head count, the two men were missing."

"We need to talk to everybody, look into the backgrounds of every person on the scene."

"Which would have been hard to do then, given the panic."

"Did anyone they were trying to rescue die?"

"No," Logan said.

He and Jace walked to the riverbank. A temporary military-looking bridge had been erected in place of the original damaged one. Traffic was moving along, and most of the bridge debris had disappeared. The vehicles had been removed from the river too.

Jace watched the water flow. Although much calmer, some serious power remained in that river.

Logan said, "According to the police reports, the men went in around here, and their bodies were dragged out farther down."

As they walked, they could see large boulders barely breaking through the top of the water. But, if they were covered by rushing water, nobody would know they were there. If the men hit one …

"When a rushing river rises and becomes a torrential flow, anybody in the flow of the current will bounce from rock to rock." Jace shook his head. "It would be hard to save anyone, even themselves."

While here, they took photos of the river's geography.

"We need photos from the accident scene. Photos from or of the crew who went into the river. Or from bystanders. And the weather reports to get a better idea of how chaotic this area was at the time."

"You can probably find all that on the internet," Logan said drily. "Nobody ever seems to give a damn what they put up there."

"It's easy to see how this could've been murder and passed off as an accident."

They walked back to their vehicle and got inside. As Jace pulled out, he saw an older woman sitting off to the side. He parked again and said, "I'll be back in a minute."

He walked over to where the woman sat on the opposite side of the road staring out. As he approached, she turned to him, and he could see the tears in her eyes. "Are you okay? Do you need assistance?" he asked gently.

"Nobody should ever see their child die," she whispered.

He nodded, understanding who she must be. "Was one of the two men your son?"

She nodded. "One was my son. The other was my nephew."

"I'm sorry for your loss."

She pinched her lips together and nodded. "Are you with the police?"

He shook his head. "No, I work for a security company. We're doing our own investigation into the accident."

"Forget about the damn accident. They've needed to put money into that bridge forever. We've sent letters and had all kinds of protests, but nobody's got funding for the broken bridges across the country. They've got it to spend on all kinds of war efforts and any number of other useless causes to further their own gains, but, when it comes to the infrastructure, the United States is falling apart."

Having recently read an article on the subject, he didn't add any comment, figuring it was better to stay neutral. When he was about to say something, she spoke again.

"I wish you'd investigate my son's death."

He squatted down beside her. "What do you think needs investigating?"

Her eyes shone brightly. "He was a fish. He was used to these rapids. He knew the high water. He knew the low water. I find it so hard to believe he drowned." She shook her head. "It just doesn't feel right."

The pain of loss could affect anybody's judgment. Everybody looked for answers and for someone to blame.

"His cousin was the same. Having been raised here, they were both water rats. Even if one of them accidentally drowned, no way both would've."

"My understanding is one got into trouble, and the other went to help him."

She sucked back a sob and then nodded, her gnarled fingers clenching together. "And that's about the only scenario that would make sense. Because they would help each other, no matter the cost."

"They were close?"

She wrapped her arms around herself. "They were close. They were wonderful people. The world is a much sadder place without them in it."

Jace straightened. "Any idea how many men were here at the time?"

She shook her head. "No. I heard there were a lot. She stood slowly and started to walk up the hill.

"Take care of yourself," he called up to her.

She shrugged her shoulders and said, "Why bother. He was my only child."

She kept walking, leaving Jace to stand behind in silence. After all, what could he say?

Chapter 3

HAVING SLEPT THROUGH her alarm, Emily woke late the next morning, shaking, tears rolling down her face. She'd had a rough night. In her dreams every person she knew or had ever known or could possibly ever meet was being systematically murdered. She knew a shrink would have a heyday with this nightmare. But it was hard to shake it loose. Even though she was late, she took a hot shower. She'd worked late last night, so she could take some extra time this morning if she needed it.

The shower warmed her up on the outside, but inside the chill was still there, and now she was really late. *Damn.* Plus she'd forgotten to put coffee on before her shower. She decided she'd hit a drive-through and pick up a cup on her way. They had a pot at work, but something about the office coffee never tasted right.

Dressed with her briefcase in hand, she opened the door and headed to her vehicle.

Not for the first time she wondered if it was time for a change of jobs. Her particular department investigated claims. And she was good at it and had a good success rate too. But she wasn't sure if she would still have a job if the head office ever found out she had a history with three open files. Her supervisor was keeping it quiet for her. She hadn't yet found a policy on the fourth man. Thank heavens.

She got into her secondhand Mercedes and drove out of the underground car park. On the road she took the first right, made a left, and then another right to the coffee shop. She pulled into the drive-through, ordered herself a cup of coffee and a muffin before pulling ahead to the second window to collect her purchases.

At the second window she recognized the vehicle directly in front of her. Or rather she recognized the men in the truck cab. It looked to be Jace and Logan. She gently raised a hand in greeting. Both men waved at her. They drove into the parking lot and waited for her. She hoped they had an update. Not that they'd had much time to get anywhere. She pulled up beside them, got out of her vehicle, and walked around.

They were both leaning against the front of their truck, holding their coffees. "Good morning," Jace said in a deep gravelly voice.

She flashed him a bright smile. "Well, it's morning. I'm not sure it's a good one. As I had a mostly crappy night. But, hey, I'm willing to be convinced today will be better." Her gaze slid to Logan and back again. "Any news?" she asked hopefully.

Jace shook his head. "I met the mother of the first victim pulled out of the river. She's struggling."

"Manila. Her name is Manila. She was always a very doting mother. Ronnie was her only child," Emily said. "I'm sure she must be devastated."

"Is she the beneficiary?"

"I believe his second wife and Manila are both beneficiaries."

"You're heading into the office now?" Logan asked. "Do you have copies of the policies?"

"I can get them for you. If you want to follow me there, I can give you a copy. If not, I can send you a PDF."

"We'll go to your office," Jace said. "We're out running errands as it is. It's easy to pick that up too."

She returned to her car, calling over her shoulder, "See you there in a few minutes." She hopped back inside and drove off.

When she arrived, Wilson was at the front door. Almost as if he was waiting for her. She hurried toward him. "Sorry I'm late."

He shrugged. "You work longer and harder than anybody else. If you're a little late, it's not a big deal."

"Thanks, I appreciate that. I had a terrible night."

"I didn't have a bad night, but the kids this morning …" Wilson sighed. "Anyone who has a family in this day and age …" He rolled his eyes at her.

She chuckled. "And you love them dearly."

"Did you write the check for the Ronnie Williamson case?"

"Not yet."

"Any reason why?"

"I'm waiting to see if the investigation reveals anything."

"Unless the wife or mother is involved in Ronnie's death, which I doubt is the case, no need to wait. They still split the insurance benefits."

"Yes, but it's an ongoing investigation." She studied him. "I guess I was looking for closure first on their different cases before we paid out," Emily said.

"The company won't be very happy if you write four checks in the amount of one million dollars all on the same day," he said jokingly. "Keep that in mind."

She sighed. "They wouldn't be happy if I wrote four

one-dollar checks on the same day," she said gently. "To be honest, insurance companies are not fond of paying out no matter the amount."

"Maybe but with good reason. It's very hard to collect the money if need be once it's paid out."

"Exactly why I was waiting. I don't think Manila or Rose had anything to do with it. But my instincts are telling me to wait."

He shot her a sharp look. "In that case, wait. Your instincts haven't let you down yet."

As she walked to her cubicle, she wondered what her instincts were telling her about Jace. That man's voice was doing things to her psyche that she hadn't felt in a long time. Yet the last thing she wanted right now was a relationship. Not when she was mentally and emotionally saying goodbye to three men she'd cared about. But it was hard to ignore Jace. Especially when she was as interested as she was.

The man was dynamite.

But was that a good thing for her?

As if reading her thoughts, Jace walked down the hall toward her, his walk determined, his gaze focused on her face.

"That was fast."

He raised an eyebrow. "We followed you."

She nodded. "My desk is over here." She glanced around. "Are you alone?"

"Logan is downstairs."

She motioned to her visitor's chair. "Take a seat." She brought up the folder with the paperwork he wanted. She quickly sent the document to the printer, then walked to the big office unit all the staff shared. She pulled the sheets from the printer, returned to her desk, and held them out. "Here you go."

He took a look. "Have you contacted any of the fami-lies?"

She nodded as she sat. "Of course. We have to deal with the families of the owner of the policy and the beneficiary."

"In this case they are the same group of people."

She glanced up and caught an odd look in his eye. She frowned at him. "What?"

"I meant, have you contacted any of the families person-ally?"

She wrinkled her nose. "I want to. I don't know what I'd say. The fact that I work for the insurance company makes it that much more awkward."

"Have you been to the accident scene?"

She felt a whisper of pain through her spine to her toes. "No. But I want to go. I should contact Manila." She sighed. "The money will never compensate for the loss of her son."

"No, it won't." Jace stood. "I'll update you when I know something." He turned and walked out.

She watched him saunter away, the walk of a man accus-tomed to command. A man capable with purpose. His loose-limbed walk moved at a steady pace. Forward toward his goal, not racing toward it and careful not to miss any details along the way. He'd probably make a hell of an insurance investigator.

Still, now that he'd mentioned it, she wanted to visit the river and see the accident site for herself.

"DID YOU LEARN anything interesting?" Logan asked as the two men walked to the vehicle. "We could've gotten a digital copy without stopping here."

Jace glanced at Logan. "Except she's one of the suspects. And we need to know what she's like."

Logan raised an eyebrow. "You think she had something to do with these murders?"

"We don't know they are all murders yet, but she has a connection to all four. If something is going on, chances are it has something to do with her."

"Still, you weren't in there more than ten minutes. What could you possibly find out?"

"She's got stacks and stacks of files on either side of her desk. She handles difficult cases. She doesn't close anything until she's gone through it thoroughly. And she's dedicated."

Logan glanced at him. "That's a big assessment for the few minutes you were in there."

"I also heard two other staff members talking about her as I walked past. Something about her being promoted because she was one of those zealots on the job."

Logan snorted. "In other words, she did her job, and the others didn't, so that pissed them off." He drove this time, directing the vehicle out of the lot. "Let's head to the street where the last two died. It's not far from here."

They drove in silence until they were a few blocks away from the accident site. Out of the blue, Logan said, "And then there's the fact that you really like her."

"What's not to like?" Jace countered. "But I don't need the headache of a relationship and never with someone involved in a case."

"I think we all thought that at the beginning. But not anymore."

"The men in her life die," Jace said. "Not sure I want to sign up for that."

That startled a laugh out of Logan. He glanced at Jace to

see if he was joking.

Jace gave him a flat stare in response. "Yes, I'm joking but maybe not."

Logan rolled his eyes. "Or there's another reason to clear her of all this mess. Then maybe you can move on with that attraction between you two."

"I don't think she knows what she wants on her side."

"Four people she knew just died. I doubt she's looking, thinking, or feeling anything at the moment other than shock and grief."

"She's grieving but doesn't know how. She feels guilty, and she doesn't think she has the right."

"How do you know that?" Logan asked. "Man, you were only in there for a few minutes."

"She had the map of the river with the accident site up on one of her monitors. She had the file open, showing the location where the two men drowned."

"You think she'll head out to each of them?"

"I think she feels it will help her solve the case. If only to reassure herself that she had nothing to do with any of this."

"That makes sense," Logan said.

"It doesn't mean she'll find anything though. And that could be because there is nothing to find."

"You believe that?" Logan asked as he pulled onto Lyle and Sicily's street. "I don't see how the deaths of four men, all cousins, couldn't be related. I suspect somebody farther down the family tree. Individuals will slowly die off once the life insurance policies are paid out. Leaving one person a total of four million dollars, if not more, the richer."

Jace whistled, the sound echoing inside the car. "That's a very long game. Most people don't have the patience for that. They kill one person and get one million dollars, and they're good."

"Only for a little while until the killing links directly to them. What if they are killing off family members so someone else inherits? Either to help them with the plan or to get the money from them later?"

"And how do we know the whole family is into this insurance stuff?" Jace shook his head. "No way to know anything for sure yet."

"If you get a strong patriarch who believes in life insurance, his beliefs pass to the extended families." Logan shrugged. "Hence you get families with several members having life insurance."

"Plus term life insurance is a sure bet and less expensive than all the rest. I mean, you expect a payout for your beneficiary, unless you commit suicide. Whereas with home and car insurance, you're betting against the house, paying out all that money monthly in case you have one future disaster."

The two men got out of the truck and walked up the block, passing the two accident scenes, their gazes constantly shifting. This was suburbia with one million streets like this in the States. Cookie-cutter homes, cookie-cutter lives.

They knocked on the neighbor's door to the left of Lyle's house. They moved to the next one over and then split up and knocked on the houses on both sides. No one was home. Jace finally found somebody at home in the third house to the right. An elderly lady answered, but she hadn't seen or heard anything. He wasn't sure she could hear well. At the end of a very frustrating but short conversation, she closed the door in his face, leaving him waiting and wondering just what had happened.

Shaking his head, he turned and walked down the street.

Typical of a suburban community like this, both spouses worked in Austin and commuted home. They all slept here, but nobody worked here because no work was to be had. Jace tried a few more houses but found them empty. When he walked back toward Lyle's house, he met up with Logan again. "Nobody's home," Jace said. "One elderly lady answered her door but was of no help."

"Did you knock on the wife's door?"

Jace shook his head. "A white SUV is in the driveway. So I'll assume she's not only home but she has company."

They quickly jotted down the license plate number, then got back into their truck.

Jace said, "That could be anybody though. She just lost a husband. She could have a sister or friend visiting."

"Yes, but isn't she also the one who Emily found in her fiancé's bed?"

"You think she's sleeping around already?" Jace frowned. It wouldn't surprise him if that was the case, but somehow humanity still managed to surprise him. "And the vehicle belongs to …" Jace spoke mainly to himself as he opened his laptop, brought up the license plate number, and read out loud, "Jimmy Burton. Age thirty-four. He's an accountant."

"Any relationship to the wife?"

"Looking …" He shook his head. "Not that I can see. He was married for two years and divorced last year."

"And Lyle's wife?"

"According to the reports Ice gave us, she has a high school education but doesn't work. She's a stay-at-home wife. Probably the only one on the block."

"And my mind immediately wonders what she's doing with so much time on her hands."

"Exactly. Yet we could be completely wrong." Jace

turned on the engine. "I suggest we see the detective and get an update."

"Already sent him a text. Waiting to hear back."

Then Jace's phone rang. "Ice, what's up?"

"I spoke with the coroner about the third and fourth victims. He's finalizing his reports now but gave me the heads-up."

"And?"

"The third victim, Lyle Cowichan, had severe head trauma. The vehicle compounded that. The report confirms the victim was dead before the vehicle ran over him. The fourth victim, Richard Manton, was drowned. Water was found in his lungs. Even though he was found dead in his car."

Jace turned to look at Logan. "The fourth victim was drowned." He pulled back into traffic. "This is getting weirder and weirder."

Chapter 4

AS SOON AS Jace left, Emily couldn't get the idea out of her mind to visit the site of the two men's drowning. She often went out in the field for things related to work. But this time it was personal. She considered asking for a day or two off work, but they were swamped. And seriously so. Now was not a good time.

It was never a good time for a death in the family, though they were no longer family. She'd had no contact with them since she broke off the relationships with each of the three men. Although she hurt for the family, those weren't close deaths as far as the company was concerned. But that didn't mean it wasn't well within the scope of her job to take a look at the accident site. She burrowed deeper into the files. The more work she got done the better. She could leave early if she got something more accomplished.

By the time she lifted her head, it was late already. She groaned and looked outside. Being summertime, the sun was still above the trees. It'd probably take close to an hour to get to the river location. She didn't want to leave it until tomorrow. She shut down her computer, got up, grabbed her purse, and walked out.

She waved at Wilson, who was still in his office, talking on the phone. He looked like he was having a hard time. Often these late-in-the-day phone calls came from the head office.

She knew the company had taken some serious hits with all the flooding across the state. And it would continue for months. Still she couldn't do anything but churn through the paperwork as fast as she could. They had investigators going from place to place, looking at the damage and sending in reports. Other staff processed those as well. But she was the one with the suspicious cases.

She hadn't talked to Ice yet, but, after seeing Jace this morning, she figured there wasn't anything important to report or Ice would have contacted Emily herself.

First she drove toward Lyle's house. It only took fifteen minutes to get through traffic. She parked on the same street, got out, and walked. Bloodstains remained on the pavement where he'd supposedly been run over. She stood and stared. Thinking that she'd almost married him was even more upsetting.

She turned to study the house where he'd lived with Sicily. It was a simple clone of the houses on either side. She'd never thought he'd like that style of home. But then she hadn't expected him to be enthralled with the idea of that whole marriage scenario either, yet he'd proposed to her out of the blue and with great enthusiasm. She didn't know when he had decided she wasn't enough and that his current wife was a much better pick. His decision had certainly turned her off of marriage. He, on the other hand, had jumped into it quickly, and they'd managed six months of wedded bliss. She was happy for him. Glad to hear he'd been happy at the end. For a time there, she'd been anything but happy.

She had been devastated and angry. How did one handle coming home to find her fiancé in bed with a strange woman? She'd gone downstairs and made coffee. The girlfriend had walked out with a big smirk on her face. Her fiancé had come down and apologized profusely. When she didn't give in, he swore at her. Called her names. Said it was her fault. She shook her head at the memory. According to him, she was the unreasonable one. If that was what made her unreasonable, then she'd accept that.

The fact that he was several steps out of sync with reality wasn't something he was prepared to look at. But after he'd done some screaming, then he'd calmed down and asked for a few of his things that were still in her house. She'd left those out on the front step. Not wanting to stay there—thankfully it was a rental, with a month-to-month lease—she'd packed up and moved to an apartment. The bad memories were too much for her.

She turned her gaze to the neighborhood, then brought out her camera and took several images. A vehicle was parked in the driveway of his house. She walked past it and took an image, capturing the license plate and the make and model. If she could do one thing for him, it was to make sure his insurance was paid out correctly. He'd always been a big one for insurance. Maybe that could have been some of the attraction he'd felt toward her.

Did he have any inkling he would die so young?

She wasn't up to talking to Sicily, Lyle's widow, right now. If ever. As it was, Emily didn't want Sicily to see her walking up and down the street. She had every right to be here, but that wouldn't make Sicily feel any better. And Emily wasn't here to cause trouble. She was here to make sure there was no trouble.

Back in her vehicle she sat in the driver's seat, pulled up her notes, and jotted down the thoughts coming to her. The vehicle in the driveway bothered her. She already knew Sicily was a cheater, so Emily had to wonder if another boyfriend was already in the mix.

As she watched, Sicily, still as pretty as ever, came outside with a young man in tow. At the SUV he bent down and kissed her gently on the lips, got into the vehicle, and drove away.

"Wow. Now that is interesting."

She shook her head and watched as Sicily stood, her fingers on her lips, staring after the vehicle. Then her gaze swept the area as if looking to see if anybody was watching. Instinctively Emily shrank down in her seat so she couldn't be seen.

After a moment, Sicily turned and walked back inside. Emily jotted down the date, the woman's actions, then started the car. In the back of her mind she wondered if this case was even related to the two drowning cases. Or had Sicily wanted to be free again? As well as gain a nice chunk of change at the same time?

Emily would look into the case a little further.

Next she headed to the river where the two cousins had lost their lives. She drove to the parking lot near one of the entrances to the path along the river. She wasn't exactly sure where the accident happened, but, as soon as she got onto the path, she could see it easily enough. Scars still ran alongside the road from where the vehicles had gone into the river. Although the water had receded in many areas, the river was wider than normal, and the path had been washed away or was still underwater. She stood in awe of the power of Mother Nature. So much water was still here.

"Those poor men."

She slowly walked along the new path created by the

many people who had been to this area. It wasn't anywhere near safe, but it was up out of the water and back a foot or two.

As she stared at the water, she realized that even being a strong swimmer wouldn't have helped if they got caught up in any of the debris in the river. It wasn't a nice thought, but she knew it happened all too often. These brave souls gave their lives to help others without a thought that they might be the ones who needed saving.

As she viewed the devastation, her mind crept forward to consider murder. Such a horrible thought. Especially in this case. Why would anybody do something like that to two volunteers here to help others?

It made no sense. She knew that humans were often twisted and what she thought people should be doing was not even on their radar. She wasn't one to see the bad side of people, but it came with her career.

That somebody might have killed two unpaid rescuers … boggled her mind.

Up ahead was a lone woman, sitting on a large rock. Emily's steps faltered. Was it her? She hadn't seen Manila in a decade.

As Emily approached, the woman looked up and frowned. Her gaze went back to the river. Emily couldn't help but feel she was intruding. As she walked closer, she asked, "Excuse me, are you Manila?"

The woman turned slowly to look at her, and she nodded. "I am. Who are you?"

Emily gave her a small smile and introduced herself. "Ronnie was my husband a long time ago, for a short while after high school."

Manila didn't just smile, all her wrinkles reformed into a

breathtaking look. "Emily? How lovely to see you. Ronnie was so happy when he was with you."

At that Emily smiled. "We were happy. We were young, and, for a while, we were happy."

The smile fell off Manila's face.

"I'm sorry for your loss, Manila," Emily said, sitting next to Manila and squeezing her hand. "I came because I found it so hard to believe they are gone. Both were such strong men."

Manila shook her head. "It shouldn't have happened. They knew these waters like no one else. They grew up swimming in the river. They only became close as adults, but, once that bond was forged, … they were like brothers."

"I'm so sorry."

For a long moment the two women sat in silence, staring at the water that had taken their loved ones away. Finally Manila stood and said, "I have to go home. These old bones of mine don't like the water as much anymore."

Emily hesitated, wondering if she should say something to her. "Did the police talk to you about the accident at all?" she asked before Manila turned away.

Manila nodded. "They asked a few questions but not much. I spoke to a man earlier, told him it couldn't have been an accident. That I wanted somebody to find the truth. And I'm afraid nobody can tell the truth because, when there's a killer, he usually is as dark and deep and silent as these rivers."

"Why would anybody want to kill those two men?" Emily asked softly, barely keeping her tears back.

Manila raised her eyes, displaying an ageless despair. "I don't know. I can't think of any reason except jealousy, rage, and greed." On that odd note, she turned and slowly walked back up the hill.

Emily could only stand and stare, tears in her eyes. *Please let these men not have met foul play. That would be so much more painful for this family to bear.*

AS JACE AND Logan drove back to the hotel later that night, their headlights shone bright in the darkness outside. Jace picked his foot off the gas pedal as he headed into a curve. "This job seems like it'll be more of a paper chaser."

Logan snorted. "This isn't the type of job we usually get, working with Levi and Ice. But, yeah, a paper-chasing job isn't for me at all. Ice, Sierra, and Sienna will have a heyday with this one."

"Maybe," Jace said thoughtfully. "We need to talk to somebody from TxSAR, see if there's any chance these men could've been murdered in front of the rest of the team."

"That's the part that bugs me. If they were all together as a group, surely somebody would've seen something. I hate to say it, but I'm thinking it must be another male—and most likely one of the other volunteer members."

"I was trying to avoid thinking about that. It goes against the grain to think that somebody would kill another team member."

"But just because we're all close, we've still seen other units that did not jive well. And often one person was at odds with everyone."

"That's true enough. But, more often than not, we were at odds with the brass, not with each other," Jace joked.

Logan nodded. "Ice will have a connection within TxSAR. We have to find out who was at the scene and interview them ourselves."

"That's tomorrow's agenda."

Jace's phone rang. Keeping an eye on the road, he pulled it from his pocket and checked to see who it was. He handed his cell over to Logan. "I don't recognize the number. Answer it for me?"

Logan put the phone on Speaker and said, "Hello, who's there?"

"Who is this?" Emily said, her voice suspicious.

Logan shot Jace a wicked grin. "It's Logan. Jace is driving, but the phone is on Speaker, so he can hear you."

"Emily, what's up?" Jace asked. He let a silly grin slip out. It was dark, and nobody could see it anyway. Besides it was good to hear that voice. If she ever went into sales, she'd make a killing.

"I just left the river site. I talked to Manila. She seems to think something is wrong here."

"I know. I spoke to her myself. Remember? Yet she had no evidence of any wrongdoing."

"Maybe but that doesn't mean there isn't any to find."

She hung up before Jace could say anything else. Under his breath he whispered, "Damn."

"That voice of hers …" Logan said.

"I know." Jace grinned. "Now what?"

The two glanced at each other, and Logan shrugged. "We wait … again."

"So much of what we do is waiting."

"But when the action hits, it hits hard and fast," Logan said in a delighted tone. "Best damn job ever."

Jace chuckled. "I can't argue that."

"You haven't been doing this for very long. Neither have I, but I'll tell you. Rhodes, Merk, and Stone started with Levi, and it's been rock 'n' roll since day one."

Jace liked the sound of that. To have the same team you cared about being at your side when you helped the rest of the world, well, a lot to be said for that. "You like being a hero," he said to Logan.

At that Logan snorted. "Don't let Levi hear you say that."

"Too late. I mentioned something about it on the first day. Hadn't realized it was such a taboo word."

"The women love it," Logan said. "Levi is not so hot on it. He's afraid he's turned the compound into a matchmaking service."

"Well, there is a hell of a lot of partnering at the compound."

"Yes, but Michael found his outside the compound." Logan grinned as he looked at Jace. "And she's not living there either. Mercy's got a place in town, so he's been back and forth."

"The last discussion I heard, he bought the land next door to the compound, is building a house for him and Mercy, plus has rented a house in the town closest to the compound. So they could stay at either place, both commuting a few minutes either way."

"Makes sense. Michael would find it very hard to be caged in with everyone else living in the same house on the compound," Jace admitted.

"He's also trying to sell off his old place. Once he gets that deal done, he'll be in a position to turn around and buy something much bigger," Logan added. "I know that Levi would like to keep him close."

"Michael was part of my unit. As was Tyson."

"And Rory too, right?"

Jace glanced at Logan. "What do you know about

Rory?"

"Levi's looking for men to tap. Michael suggested he ask Rory."

"Rory would be good. And, yeah, he's one of my old unit too. They're all good men."

Logan nodded. "That's how we all feel. At this point, Levi has more ex-military than any other company going."

"That's because he's easy to deal with. It's work that we love to do, that we're trained to do, and that we're good at." He shrugged. "A marriage made in heaven. But, if any of those women start decorating that damn place with wedding bells, I'm getting the hell out of there."

"You know? That's one thing that hasn't happened yet. There's been lots of talk of partnering. But nobody's mentioned marriage. I'm waiting for the first woman to get pregnant."

"Can you imagine the compound full of kids?" Jace said. "It boggles the mind."

"Alfred would be in heaven."

"Maybe. But our lifestyle is hardly conducive to family living."

"No. But the compound is as close to that as I think we'll ever get. Everyone safe, happy, and well loved. Lots of properties around the compound. Those who want their own space can have it," Logan said. "Not everybody needs to be there. I spend a lot of time on my dad's estate because he's aging."

Jace pulled up outside the hotel. "Anna's business is getting bigger and bigger all the time," he commented. "It's pretty amazing the kind of animal rescue work she does."

"I know. My father and Levi both contribute to the place on a regular basis."

"That's good to know. It's a worthy cause," Jace said. "I know there was talk about building some more pens or something for her this weekend."

"If we're not still working this case, yes. But chances are, you and I will still be in Austin, working."

"I'm all for that. But, if I'm home, I like to be busy too."

"You won't have to say that twice. Something always needs to be done. I think Alfred's even talking about a garden now. So, if you open your mouth at the wrong time, you can be doing all kinds of shit work."

Jace grinned. "You know? That doesn't sound half bad. As a matter of fact, it sounds damn good."

Chapter 5

J ACE AND LOGAN were at the insurance office door, waiting for Emily as she joined them outside. She checked her watch. "You guys are early."

"Not really. We've been up for hours."

"You could have called me on my cell," she said.

Logan smiled. "Well, we tried. You didn't answer."

She shot him a surprised look, pulled out her cell phone, and winced. "Wow. With everything going on, I forgot to charge it." She shoved it back into her pocket. "I have a spare charger in my office."

"In that case, I presume this is a habit?"

She shook her head. "No, but then I'm in the field a lot, so it's handy to have a charger at the office and at home."

"Maybe you should get one for the vehicle," Jace said slowly.

She shrugged, unlocked the front door, surprised Wilson wasn't in already. She motioned the two men inside in front of her. "Now that you're here, let's go find out what the problems are."

They walked upstairs to her office. "Are you always the first one in?" Jace asked.

She shook her head. "No. I'm not." She checked her watch again. "I'm only a few minutes early. I expect every-body else will be in soon. Coffee?"

"Yes, please," Logan said.

She glanced over at Jace. He nodded. She liked that about him. He was a man of few words, a relief after the chatty lot she had in her line of business. She put on a pot. When it was done dripping, she poured three cups and motioned to the two men. "Fix it the way you like. Let's work in the boardroom." She watched as both men picked up the cups of black liquid and turned to face her. She shook her head. "Of course you like it strong and black." She led the way to the boardroom. When they were all inside, she closed the door. "Okay, so what is it you need?" She grabbed the closest chair and sat down.

"Check the policies paid out to anyone in the family or anyone in the TxSAR group."

"Great, how many more people?" she asked with a sigh. "I still haven't completed the family tree as it is."

"Ice sent a short list this morning." Logan brought up his cell and opened the list.

She read through the names. "None of them sound familiar. Who are they?"

"TxSAR personnel who have died in the last twenty years."

"Why twenty years?"

"It's how long that office has been in operation."

She turned to stare at him. "You're thinking it's more to do with TxSAR than the extended family?"

"We won't leave any rock unturned."

"Email it to me, will you, please?" She brought out a notepad and wrote things down. "I can get the information for you, but it'll take some time."

"Do you have anybody to help you?" Jace asked.

"I can assign somebody. But, so far, I've kept my mouth

closed because I'm associated with the four of them. Don't get me wrong," she added hurriedly, holding out her hands. "I'm certainly not hiding it, and my boss knows, but I don't believe he's told the head office at this time."

"Can he help you?"

She smiled. "He's a manager for a reason. He doesn't do very much of the hands-on work."

Jace nodded. "Can you slough off any of your other work so this becomes a priority?"

"It is my priority," she said calmly. "But it's not as simple as typing the name into the database. These names are not necessarily the names on the policies. People marry, get divorced. They change their names. … Nobody ever thinks to update an insurance policy."

Jace sat back with a surprised look on his face. "That makes sense."

"Like a painting, we need to have a paper trail to follow," she said. "It has to be legal. They have to prove they are who they say they are before we write a check."

"Will that paper trail be in the archives?" Logan asked.

She glanced at him. "It's likely to be in the notes. But, if some of these records go back twenty years, … we didn't have digital records back then. We'll find scanned documents and old paper documents with notes written as well as they could've been. But there could be gaps in the information. I will do what I can. Also I promised Ice that I would look for other family members. It would be helpful if we knew from the family themselves who might have an insurance policy because I represent only one of many insurance companies. It would make sense to think that some would have insurance policies with other companies."

"And yet, if they didn't, then that would be another line

to tug because then the insurance company would also be a common denominator."

"That's possible. I don't think it's very likely. Insurance companies are very competitive. So there are many reasons for somebody to come to our company versus another one."

"Unless someone in the family either worked in the company or knew somebody who did—other than you." Jace leaned forward, his fingers tapping the table. "We need a list of past employees, particularly fired or disgruntled ones who could have accessed the policies."

She winced. "And that could be a whole lot harder to find."

Jace gave her a flat stare. "Why is that?"

"Because that information is confidential and might need a warrant," she reminded him gently. "I'll help you as much as I can within the parameters I'm allowed. And I know Wilson will be on board to go right to the edge, but I don't know if the employee list is included in that or not." When Jace opened his mouth to protest, she held up her hand. "I will check it out and do what I can. When I know something, I'll pass it on to you. But, if you got a warrant, that would be much better."

Jace narrowed his gaze and settled back in his chair. "And we might have to, but that will be a last resort. But the faster we get information, the faster this will go."

"I need more hands," she muttered.

"While we can get the information on our own, I presume you don't want us hacking into your system," Logan said with a big grin.

Her gaze flew to him in horror. "Please don't do that. Please don't even suggest something like that, even as a joke."

"Why?" Jace asked sharply. "Has the company been hacked?"

She picked up her coffee cup and took a sip. "Before I started working here, some of our files were hacked. To this day, we're not exactly sure what was accessed. Obviously our security is much stronger now. But, at the time, nobody understood how far into our database a hacker could go."

Logan whistled low and hard. "Wow. That completely opens up the suspect list."

"Why?"

"Because now there are a lot of people who would've known who had policies and would also have the personal information as to who was related and who were the beneficiaries. This may have nothing to do with the individual family members," Jace said. "It could very well be the hackers found several policy holders within the one family and just rolled a dice to choose the next victim."

"Or they played that long game that Jace and I were talking about, and they have an end result," Logan said.

Jace nodded. "This is a very interesting element." He picked up his phone and said, "I'll send Levi and Detective Dickerson a note about this."

She reached across and covered his hand with hers. "Please try to keep this confidential. If any of this gets out to the public, the insurance company will face a horrific backlash."

He studied her face for a long moment, then nodded. "I will do what I can. But this is not information we can hide, not when four people have potentially been murdered for their policies. Someone had to know they had the policies."

Logan leaned forward and tapped her notepad. "And that means we need to know every policy handed out that the hackers accessed."

She stared at him in horror. "Do you understand how many thousands of names that is?" She shook her head. "I can get through all this stuff, but you're asking for weeks' worth of work. And that's only if the company approves this. Which I highly doubt. We need more justification for that amount of work."

Logan sat back and drummed the tabletop. "Let's start with everyone within Austin and the surrounding areas."

She glanced at him.

"Any way to narrow those fields down by profession or as TxSAR members?" Jace asked, turning to Emily.

She shook her head. "Not really. Sometimes forty years go by since the first policy was taken out, and people don't update the information when they marry or divorce. Sometimes people even forget about their policies."

"Let's think about this specifically so we can shorten the list."

"What we need is the names of beneficiaries, their addresses …" Logan said, staring off into space. "But then we also need the sex and potentially the rest of that person's family tree. What if we create a program to do that?"

"If we had the list of names, then, yes."

Jace glanced at Emily. "You can get the list of names and any of the database information that comes with it, such as the address, sex, age, and the beneficiary. Then maybe we'll take all that information and sort it into something a little more usable."

She pinched the bridge of her nose. "I have to get permission. This is confidential information."

"It's all confidential information. But the fact is, somebody's already had access to it. So we're years behind them.

They've had that long to make plans."

She tossed down her pen and raised both hands in surrender. "But this is all conjecture," she exclaimed. "We don't even know that Ronnie and Howard's deaths were anything but an accident."

"That's true. But we do know about Lyle Cowichan and Richard Manton."

She pointed a finger at him and shook it. "Those two are for the police to sort out. And we have no way of knowing who might have killed them. Even assuming Sicily knows about the life insurance—and one million dollars is hard to walk away from—thinking about something is a very different thing than doing something concrete about it. Now if she had someone to help …"

"Particularly when she already has the weapon, her ex-boyfriend."

"But we don't know that," she reminded him, yet vividly remembered the guy standing by the white SUV kissing Sicily in her driveway. Should she tell them now about that? She was an investigator and knew all possibilities should be considered. Would telling them about Sicily bring too much attention on her? God knew Emily had no reason to protect Sicily. But Emily's job was to do right by the people who bought these policies to take care of their loved ones afterward. "I understand we have to follow all these trails, but it'll take time."

"And we're here," Logan said, "to make sure that the time happens a whole lot faster than if you were left to your own devices. So get permission from your boss or from his bosses or whoever to get the list of names from all payouts before the breach and the security was boosted. You can do that without showing us the results. Then do a search of those names related to the four cousins' families. Also check Ice's list of TxSAR members killed. Depending on what you find—if you find anything—then we can see what the next step is. Obviously we need this kept aboveboard so the evidence doesn't get thrown out in court."

She sank back in her chair, holding her cup of coffee close to her chest as she studied the men. She didn't have any reason to argue, but it was a ton of work, and, maybe more than anything, she was scared. Scared of what they might find. "This could get really ugly," she said weakly.

"Depending on who's doing it, if somebody's doing it," Jace said, "it will get ugly." He shrugged. "It's not your fault. You didn't have a hand in it. And, yes, it's your workplace and your job, but no way this can be covered up. Still, we'll do what we can to keep it private. But, if we find out somebody's using the insurance company's database to access potential victims, there's no way to keep it out of the media. This can be a circus if it ever goes to trial."

She leaned back and closed her eyes. So many names swirled through her head. "I can't even imagine how many cases we've closed that I'll have to sift through if you want me to go back twenty years."

"It doesn't matter how many," Jace said gently. "We still must look at them. And with as much demographic infor-mation as you have, so we can look for patterns."

She rolled her head to the side and studied him. "You guys have computer geeks at the compound?"

"Several of them. And, even if we didn't, we have good friends who can follow through. Several programmers are within our circle of friends."

She shook her head. "We can't let anybody else into this."

"Oh, the one I'm thinking about has national defense contracts, so I'm pretty darn sure Tesla would get clearance for this."

"Not just her though. Sienna does forensic accounting. She understands the need for basic trust. Merk and Rhodes are both damned good." Logan smiled. "I'm no slouch in that department either. And, if need be, my father has an IT specialist who works for him. Everybody has top security levels."

She groaned and then finally capitulated. "I'll talk to Wilson. But I can't guarantee anything."

"No, but you'll have to convince him that we need this material." Logan pushed his chair back and stood. "This has gotten way too big to hide anymore."

Jace got up, walked to the door, and opened it for Logan to leave first. He faced Emily. "It's nine now. We'll take you out for lunch at twelve. Make sure you have that talk beforehand." He turned and walked out, flashing her a bright smile. "Might not be all that hard to do." He closed the door behind him, leaving her alone in the room.

"Not that hard," she muttered as she got up and headed to her office. "Is he nuts? Wilson'll never go for this."

Emily made it four steps when she heard Wilson's voice.

"Emily, come in. Catch me up on what's going on."

She took a deep breath, walked into his office, and plastered a smile on her face. "What's going on is, we have a much bigger problem than we first thought."

AS THE MEN drove out of the parking lot, Logan glanced at Jace and said, "You think she'll get us the information?"

"I hope so. I'm more worried the head office will give

her grief."

"Ice says that, if Emily can't make it happen, Ice might jump in there and force the company's hand."

"Well, if she can't, the police certainly can." Jace drove toward the Austin police station. "I figured we'd personally stop in and meet Detective Dickerson if he's there. See if we can get the autopsy reports on the last two victims."

"I'd like to see those too. I can't believe the fourth man drowned. He was in his goddamn car."

The police station was busy. They found parking in the back lot, then walked inside, asking to see the detective. The woman gave them a harried look and told them to take a seat. The two men exchanged glances and sat down.

Jace pulled out his phone and sent a message to the detective. *We're in the waiting room. If you have a moment, we could use a ten-minute conversation.* He hit Send, then pocketed his phone. When he looked up, a man strode toward him.

He approached with his hand out. "I'm Detective Dickerson. I presume you're both here to see me."

Jace and Logan stood, shook the man's hand, and Jace said, "Were you expecting us?"

He nodded. "Ice said you'd be here this morning."

Jace smiled. "You've got to appreciate it when somebody paves the way for you."

"You know Ice?" Logan asked the detective.

"Absolutely. We've worked on several local cases that have come up. She's a good person. Any help she can give us right now is huge. Although I have to admit that I'm not exactly sure what we're looking at in this case."

With Logan sending him a warning look, Jace realized that the PD waiting area wasn't the best location to go over these details. "Sounds like we need a place to talk quietly. You can fill us in on what you found."

Detective Dickerson was clearly hoping this would go the other way. He exchanged a look with Logan.

Logan shrugged. "Not exactly sure what we've found yet. Ice might be the better person to tell you that."

The detective snorted. "No hedging." He motioned to a small room with a table in the center and several chairs around it. "Let's talk in here." He shut the door behind them.

When they were seated, the detective said, "I have the autopsy results on Richard Manton. And on Lyle Cowichan." He held up two folders in his hand.

"We heard from our boss. She got a few details from the coroner. None of this makes sense," Jace said. "Nobody drowns in their car after an altercation in which the other party was run over by a vehicle."

The detective laughed. "I wondered that myself. The autopsy put the two men's deaths within the same hour. But the medical examiner can't come any closer than that."

"How was Richard found?" Jace asked.

Detective Dickerson looked at the papers in his file and said, "His vehicle was parked down the block. Nobody checked it out because it had smoky windows. It was only when the vehicle sat there for a long time that a neighbor came out, took a closer look, and realized somebody was inside. She called 9-1-1. She did not open the vehicle and didn't touch the car, she says."

"So we have two men fighting at a barbecue. Then one man is run over, but he's dead already, and I suppose it was made to look like a hit-and-run accident. But he's already bearing the marks from the fight. The second man, also bearing the marks of the fight, drowns in his vehicle. So are we to assume that somebody poured water into his lungs?"

"Correct. Abrasions were found on the inside of his throat, as if a funnel had been shoved down it, and water poured in it."

"Not exactly an easy thing to do if the person was conscious. So we assume he was unconscious. Still not something that's easy to do if people are watching."

"Yes. Now the barbecue was later on a Saturday. There wasn't any traffic on that small side street. If somebody had been standing and talking to the driver for a certain amount of time, people might've noticed but looked away. It still would have taken luck on the killer's part to have done this without any witnesses."

"Or potentially Lyle, instead of going to his room, went to the garage or some secluded place, where he attacked his attacker, poured the water into the man's lungs, helped him somehow to his vehicle, and then, when he left the vehicle, he fell into the road and died from previous injuries and was struck by another vehicle."

"As in karma?"

The detective shrugged. "I've certainly seen a lot of weird things in my line of work, so that wouldn't surprise me. But again how does he get the man into the vehicle, and, if he drove the car down the block, he still would have to move the now dead man into the driver seat. Also not easy. Although …" He tapped the autopsy report. "Lyle Cowichan was six feet and an easy 240 pounds. Richard Manton was only five eight and 150 pounds." The detective settled back with a smile. "I like it."

"Now all you have to do is get the rest of the evidence to back that up," Logan said drily.

The detective nodded with a laugh. "That's a trick. As always." He leaned forward. "I can give you guys a copy of these autopsy reports. I want to know anything you find as it comes available."

"That we can do."

"Ice said this might be connected to another case," Detective Dickerson said. "She didn't want to go into any details yet because she wasn't sure." He glanced at the folder in his hand. "Honestly I have a million other cases I'm dealing with. But, if it is connected, I need to know fast."

Jace stood. "Hopefully we will have information for you in the next few days."

The detective's eyebrows rose. "Now that would be good. I won't get this case closed for weeks yet. Still waiting to hear back from forensics on fingerprints and fibers from the vehicle. Both men had DNA from the other man under their own fingernails, but we're still looking to see if a third party figures in. It's quite possible someone ran over the one and then turned his attention to the other one."

"Unfortunately, yes." Logan shook his hand. "We'll see ourselves out."

Jace nodded to the detective. "Thanks for seeing us so quickly."

The detective watched as the two men left. Jace could feel Dickerson's gaze burning on his back. "I like that theory," he said to Logan as soon as they stepped outside. "The thing is, it's just a theory. Until there is evidence to support it."

"And why drowning? Is that the faster, easier method to kill a man? If he's unconscious already, why not smother him, break his neck, beat his head in? All are much easier than trying to drown an unconscious man."

"He was in the vehicle. He could have broken his neck if he had to carry him anyway. The water must have significance."

"Now that segues us back to the first two men who drowned," Logan said.

Chapter 6

EMILY SAT DOWN and said to her boss, "You okay?"

He nodded. "I'm running behind," he fussed. "I have a conference call in fifteen minutes." He stared at the coffee in her hand. "I didn't get coffee at the house this morning."

"Too many kids to hug and kiss."

The smile beamed across his face. "Something like that. I got peanut butter on my shirt collar as their arms were around my neck and had to rush and change my shirt."

She chuckled. "And yet that would've been adorable."

"If the timing hadn't been so tight, it would've been. As it is …"

"You're not late."

"I don't like being pressed for time." He placed his arm on his desk and looked at her. "Now, what can I do for you?"

She launched into an explanation of her meeting with Jace and Logan. The look of horror that crossed Wilson's face would've made her laugh if it wasn't such a serious subject.

"You told him about that security breach?"

She leaned forward. "I had to tell him. They are digging deep into things. They'd find out and how would that look? It's bad enough that we didn't tell the police way back when." She settled back as he sputtered. "We also must prepare for the fact that, if Legendary Security finds anything further, this could definitely become a police issue."

Wilson shook his head rapidly. "No. You don't understand. We can't have that." He looked at her expectantly as if she could make it all magically go away.

"When somebody hacked our accounts, if they used that information to kill people for insurance money, we have no choice." She enunciated the last part clearly, trying to get through the fantasy look on her boss's face that said she could fix anything. "I can't fix that."

Wilson wasn't listening. "I have faith in you." He turned on his computer as if to say the conversation was over.

She groaned. "I need your permission to pull that information and give it to them."

He gave her a harried look. "Why?"

"I explained why," she said patiently. "I'm not authorized to hand out that information. You are."

He got a hunted look around the edges of his eyes. "And, if this goes south, then I go south with it," he complained. "What if I lose my job?"

"Neither of us can afford to lose our jobs," she said gently. "But the fact is, the head office won't be impressed if the police come in here with warrants and gain access to all this anyway. The fallout with the media would be horrific."

He sagged in place. "I'll talk to my boss about it."

She could see he was more stressed out than when he first arrived. She stood to leave. "And do it this morning. The men are coming back at noon for my answer."

He waved at her. "Go away."

She turned and walked out of the office. "If you don't get the clearance, then Ice will get it for us."

He gave her a look. "Who's Ice?"

Emily smiled. "You probably don't want to know if

you're the one stopping her from getting what she needs to get."

His shoulders hunched a bit more. "Shut the door behind you."

She closed it with a sharp *click* and walked back to her desk. Some things she could do without the required permission. But no way would she get very far before the men showed up at lunchtime. She settled down with a large mug of coffee, a clean sheet of paper open on her notepad, and went through the names on Ice's list. Maybe she could compile them into a shorter list. She had a ton of open cases too. But the system here wasn't exactly set up in a way she could move them to somebody else's desk. When folders got added to her load, others never got removed.

Hoping for an easier place to start, she worked on the men's names first, as men were less likely to change their surnames than women.

The first three men on the list had no policies. Several policies popped up with their surnames but without the correct first names. On her notepad she wrote down the last names. She was afraid she'd have to go back and search a little deeper when Ice got this information. That's when she realized these men were still alive. Ice was looking to possibly prevent another murder. Talk about pressure. With four men dead in a short amount of time, Emily had no way to know how many others had already been taken out. And that massive twenty-year-long list she was expecting from Jace would be in her hands soon. One couldn't deal with so many variables at the same time.

Staying focused, by the time she got to the last one, she had several sheets of notes. Four of the names had policies. Two of those had died with a policy in place with her company. The number of the payout made her queasy. It was one million dollars again.

She rubbed her temples. "That was normal though."

A lot of policies were for one million, half a million, some only one hundred thousand dollars. It brought to mind the possibility that somebody was searching for million-dollar payouts and killing the people involved. Talk about a horror movie. For the two with policies still active, she wrote down the beneficiaries and then the other information, keeping in mind what Jace had said this morning. She added in age, religion, address, and any other information in the notes she deemed potentially informative.

In both cases, the insurance money went to their spouses. She quickly found the last man's policy. He was alive but his wife had passed away. Emily made a mental note that somebody needed to contact the man and change who his beneficiary was. No point in paying for a policy if nobody received the insurance proceeds. With that taken care of, she opened up her email document and transferred all her notes into her computer and saved a copy. Then she contacted Ice by email and sent her the list. An email came back a few moments later.

Thanks. I'll get back to you if I have any more questions.

As she closed the email, Emily realized something about one of the policies they had paid out that bothered her. She checked into the policy for Ken Foster. His had been a half-million-dollar payout, which was a break from the others. And the beneficiary had been his wife. There had been no questions; the payment had been made. What made her stomach queasy was he had died on a rescue—he had drowned. When her phone rang a moment later, she wasn't surprised to see the caller ID.

"Morning, Ice," she said in a low voice. She was at the back corner of the building, and, although she was in a cubicle and didn't have anybody too close to her, she spoke softly.

"Good morning, Emily. Thank you very much for the information. I do have a question."

"I gathered as much. What's the problem?"

"In your file, does it say anything about how Ken Foster died?"

Emily winced. "Yes. He drowned."

A moment of silence passed before Ice spoke. "Do you have the date when that happened?" Ice's voice was all business now.

Emily looked up the file. "Fifteen months ago on March 26."

"And is that his legal name, or did he change his name?"

"Yes, that's his legal name. And his date of birth was April 4, 1962."

"Do we have any family members for him?"

"Just a minute, I'll take a look." Emily flipped through the file, looking for notes and any attachments or indices. "I don't see anything on file."

"Okay, I'll hunt it down." And she hung up.

Emily slowly hung up her desk phone and stared at the computer in front of her. It wasn't that the cause of death was so similar to the others that made her skin crawl. But that it wasn't different enough to not be included in this whole mess. So fifteen months ago somebody was killing people for their insurance policies. Why? It wasn't like they were the beneficiary. Unless it was a Robin Hood thing, where they were stealing from the rich to give to the poor, how were these people being singled out?

Once again she had too many damn questions and not enough answers. Hating the direction of her thoughts, and the sickly feeling that she was getting from this whole nightmare, she got up and poured herself another cup of coffee and walked to the window. A river was in her view, a beautiful one with walkways on both sides. She'd always taken solace from Mother Nature's beauty. Right now all she could think about was how someone could take something so beautiful and use it as a murder weapon.

"YOU THINK EMILY will have any information ready for us?"

"She'll have some of it. She already sent Ice information on the names she'd asked for."

"She can do only so much," Logan said. "Why are we at the morgue anyway?"

Jace smiled. "Because the drowning in the vehicle sounded very odd to me."

"You think?"

They walked in through the front door. The woman at the desk gave them a surprised look and said, "What can I do for you?"

"Dr. Morgenstern is expecting me," Jace said. "I'm Jace Colley. This is Logan Redding."

She nodded, grabbed the phone, and called through. After a moment she said, "He'll be here in a moment."

The door opened, and a man in his sixties strode out with an air of narrowed no-nonsense around him. He motioned toward his office and said, "Follow me."

They followed him down the hallway. At an office, he opened the door. "Take a seat."

"Thanks for seeing us," Jace said.

"I've known Ice for a lot of years. Her father and I went to med school together."

Jace smiled. He had to love working for a company that had connections.

The doctor steepled his fingers, dropping his chin on top of them. "What's this all about?"

"We're looking into a series of deaths that could potentially be linked and could potentially be murder."

"Well, the man I have was obviously murdered. I can't imagine anybody doing this to himself. It would be impossible for a living person to shove a long gasoline funnel down one's own throat and pour water into one's own lungs, due to the gag reflex, the body's own inclination to save itself."

Logan asked, "So we can definitely rule out suicide?"

The coroner nodded. "I've seen people do some strange things to themselves. But I don't think that was the case this time. The abrasions inside his throat would've been extremely painful, even if a very small tube was used."

"Would he have needed medical training?"

The coroner frowned, tapping his fingers on the desk, and thought about it. "It certainly would help to get the funnel in the right place. But an amateur could have done it, or anybody with basic first-aid. Honestly, in this day and age, the internet gives you all the information you might want. So I can't say for sure he would have had medical knowledge. I'm just saying it would have helped. Given the presence of scrapes and abrasions, I don't think very much care was taken. It was a fast job."

"Can you analyze the water that came out of his lungs for us?"

The coroner's eyebrows shot up. "Why?"

"We want to rule out the source of water. Was it from the same river where two other TxSAR men drowned several weeks ago?"

The coroner leaned forward. "Now that's an interesting twist."

Jace shrugged. "There could be a connection. But we

can't be sure that the other two men were murdered."

"Tell me what river was involved." The coroner brought out his notepad, and also he brought up the case file on his computer. "My instinct was that it was tap water. But should this be connected, well, that would be one way to find out."

"The Blanco River is where the two men drowned several weeks ago."

The coroner looked thoughtful. "I remember that. The TxSAR men. One was assumed to have gotten into trouble, and the other went in after him to save him, and they both drowned." He narrowed his gaze sharply and stared at them. "And yet you're suspecting foul play?"

"Both men had one-million-dollar life insurance policies on their lives."

"Given their type of volunteer work, that's not uncommon," the coroner said. "Most people who flirt with danger have a fallback for their families."

Logan nodded. "Exactly. But then you have the man who was run over by a vehicle."

The coroner nodded. "He was unconscious when he fell on the street and was then run over." He leaned back and tapped his chin. "What possible connection could there be between all four of these men?"

Jace said, "There are three connections. One, they all worked as TxSAR volunteers." He glanced over at Logan.

Logan added, "They're all cousins, from the same family."

"And," Jace added, "Three had one-million-dollar life insurance policies, the fourth man had a half a million dollar plan, but all with the same company."

The coroner leaned forward, his chair hitting his desk with a bang. "Well, that does make it interesting."

Chapter 7

"Emily?"

Startled, Emily looked up from the file she was buried in. Wilson stood in front of her.

He motioned toward his office. "I need to talk to you."

She stood, snatched up her notebook, and followed him.

In his office, with the door closed, he sat down heavily and said, "I just got off the phone with the head office."

She nodded, not liking his tone of voice. No way this would be good for any of them. She hoped the company would do the right thing.

"They're insisting on a warrant before we hand out that kind of confidential information."

She sagged in place. "Are you sure?"

Wilson nodded. "It is confidential information."

She rubbed her hand on her forehead. "Then you need to know I searched the TxSAR deaths list from the last twenty years that Ice gave me and came up with information on four of them."

"What were the names, and what did you find out?"

She quickly explained.

He frowned. "Surely that's not enough to cause any concern."

"I doubt it. That's why I gave her the information." She shrugged. "I figured being cooperative would get us less trouble than not."

He sat back. "Depends. However, if the police requested it, then we have no option but to hand it over. Anyone else though …"

"If a warrant is required," she said, "I rather imagine they can get it. But, once a warrant is issued, it all becomes public knowledge."

His brows came together. "I'm not sure about that."

She nodded. "Once the media finds out a warrant has been issued, then it could be a huge circus."

"A warrant could be issued for any number of reasons," Wilson protested.

"Sure, but reputation is everything." She shrugged. "I think Ice was trying to get to the bottom of this without bringing in the police or the media. I really feel that giving Ice the information avoids all that, and they could see if there are any worrisome patterns."

He shook his head. "I can bring it up with the head office again. But, at the moment, my hands are tied."

She stood. "Then I'll pass that on." She turned and walked to the door. "And what about the information I have already given her?"

"Forward the email you sent to her so I can take a look. I can reassure those at the head office that nothing confidential was handed over."

She nodded and walked out of his office. Inside her stomach was churning. Ice needed that information. Even though Emily knew it was not the company's fault, what if the murderer had killed others?

On the other hand, what if there was no killer at all? Mentally confused and frustrated at the political wrangling, she headed back to her desk. As soon as she sat down, her cell phone rang. She pulled it out and saw Jace's name shining up at her. She smiled as she answered. "Hello."

"It's almost lunchtime. We're heading to your office to pick you up. Is ten minutes okay?"

She glanced at her monitor and realized it was indeed almost noon. "Sure, that's fine. A meal it is."

She tucked her phone into her purse, logged off her computer, grabbed her notebook, stuffed it into her bag, and headed to the ladies' room. No way she would get anything else done right now anyway. She hadn't told Ice about the company's decision. But she figured, once she told Jace and Logan, they'd pass on the news.

She walked out the front door and stood at the curb. Her stomach was growling, after missing breakfast. She thought with longing about yesterday's muffin. But she hadn't had time this morning. With the stress, her nerves were that much rougher.

When she looked down the street, she saw Jace and Logan driving toward her. Logan pulled up in front, and Jace opened the door.

He got into the back seat and said, "You take the front."

She should protest, but he was already in the back with the door shut. She rolled her eyes and scrambled into the front of the truck Shutting the door, she grabbed the seat belt and said, "So where are we going for lunch?"

Logan laughed. "It's a toss-up between Italian and the Curry House."

Her eyebrows rose. "If I have a say in the matter, I'm going with the Curry House."

Jace snorted behind her. "I told you that she'd go with my choice."

She glanced at Logan. "If you need to win this one," she

said with a big grin, "I'll be happy with Italian."

"No, that's okay," Logan said, pulling back out into traffic. "Indian it is."

The Curry House was a mile away. When they pulled into the rear parking lot, they took the last spot. "At least it's busy," Logan said. "That should mean it's good food."

"I've been here several times," she said. "It is good."

Inside the restaurant, they were shown to a table in the far back corner. That suited her. She needed to talk to the men. The least amount of people listening, the better.

When seated and their orders taken, Jace turned toward her. "How did you do this morning?"

She shrugged. "Win some and lose some."

"Let's start with the wins," Logan said.

She chuckled. "Like a kid, always wanting the good news first."

"In this business I'll take any good news first."

"So I ran the numbers and names for Ice. Four names popped up that raised some flags for her." She quickly went over the files.

The men sat back.

"Interesting that the amount of one was different."

"But not enough to discount."

"Also the fact that he drowned."

"Do we know why Ice chose those names?"

Jace shook his head. "I didn't ask."

Logan leaned forward. "What about access to the database?"

She shook her head. "The head office said no, not without a warrant."

Jace didn't say anything.

She glanced over at him. "You don't seem surprised."

He shrugged. "Bureaucracy. They do everything they can to keep things buttoned down tight."

Silence settled over the table for the next few moments. Then she said in a low voice, "What will you do?"

Jace glanced at Logan and said, "Call to see what Ice might want to do next."

"You must have a little more than wanting to check a database in order to get a warrant," she said seriously. "Do you have any real proof that there's been foul play? Or anything along that line? No judge will give it to you without evidence."

"No, maybe not," he said. "But a judge might when they realize there was a security breach, and your company didn't inform all its members that their private information had been hacked."

She stared at him in shock. "You can't do that. I'll lose my job."

Jace turned to her. "Why would you lose your job?"

"Because I told you that we had the security breach."

Then their meals arrived. She stared at the plate of lamb curry but wasn't hungry anymore. She picked up her fork and stabbed a piece of meat. "I was thinking of changing jobs anyway."

Logan chuckled. "They can't blame you."

She shot him a look. "You know they can, and they will. I'll be the fall guy."

That shut him up. She took a bite and remembered why she chose curry. This was succulent and so full of flavor.

"Why were you looking at changing your job?" Jace asked.

There was just something about that voice. So very compassionate. Adding that to the powerful sexiness, he was deadly on her senses. "Because I deal with a lot of unpleas-antness," she said. "I get all the questionable cases, those that require investigation. I have investigators out in the field all the time. I go out myself. I have a very high closing rate. And because that's what I'm good at, I get more fraud and murders than I care to work on." She took another bite of her delicious food, feeling some joy at the spices warming through her. "This was a good choice," she said. "Even if I don't like the subject matter."

"We're sorry to upset you," Jace said. "It's not our intention. But this investigation has certainly grown in scope, and that's something we can't ignore. If there is any chance of a connection to previous insurance claims, then we need to know. If it's connected to the hacking of your security data, that we also need to know. If any of the people since that data was breached has been using it for their own gain, then we need to know."

"I get it. I get it. But you know what any corporation is like. They won't hand over anything unless they have to."

Logan nodded. "But, if the information was stolen once, I'm sure a lot of it is on the internet. You might find it on your own."

She froze, her fork in midair. "Are you nuts?" she hissed.

Jace looked at her in surprise. "Barring the fact somebody may have stolen it and not sold it but kept it for himself, then it's probably sitting in a private server until the thief has a reason to use the information. Not to mention the person may have left his own security wide open or may have put something on the internet for others to follow. It's never quite as simple as stealing and not leaving any tracks. There are almost always signs of something left behind."

She felt sick to her stomach again. "So you're saying

that, even though the security breach was probably fixed, it could be vulnerable even now?"

"What I'm saying is that, even though the security might've been fixed, whoever stole that information could have left it accessible in an entirely different location. There is no way to know."

"In that case, whoever finds it would be a good hacker themselves."

"The technology has changed in the four years since you had the security breach. Your company would have boosted its security and doubled down on the encryption software available at the time. But that doesn't mean there isn't newer technology even now."

She shook her head. "We need to change the subject. I'm having trouble keeping lunch down."

The two men exchanged glances, then looked back at her.

She glared at them both. "I mean it."

And she tackled her lunch again.

JACE SMILED. HE liked a woman who wouldn't take any shit. Then again, he really liked Emily. He also liked that she cared more about the people insured than the company. It wasn't that he wasn't a company man, because, when he needed to be, he was. But, when the company was in the wrong, he didn't like blindly obeying. In this case, he understood the company's stand, but it wasn't helpful.

He didn't expect to get a warrant without further proof. She was right there. A judge would need a justifiable reason to give them access to the database.

They finished lunch and drove her back to her office.

Since she had put her foot down, the conversation had dwindled to the weather and was not helpful to their investigation.

Logan pulled up in front of her office. Jace got out, opened the door for her, and then told Logan, "I'll be back in a few minutes." He slipped his hand under her elbow and led her to the front door.

She glanced up at him. "You don't have to come in. I know you don't want to spend any more time with me than you have to."

He chuckled, the sound surprising him not only at the spontaneity of it but that it happened at all. "The business has nothing to do with you. I want to spend as much time with you as I can."

The words came out so instinctively and so smoothly, it was like he had practiced them. But inside he watched his own actions in astonishment. He'd never thought he would have said something like that before.

She glared at him suspiciously. "You think you can get more information out of me if you do?" She gave him a challenge with that.

He halted, pulling her to a stop too, and slanted his gaze down at her. "Hell no. I wouldn't want to spend time with you if you did. If morals and trust don't matter to you, then you're not the kind of person I thought you were."

"Well, I know you were not happy with me."

"It's not you I'm unhappy with. It's the company line. What I don't want to have happen is somebody else die because we can't unlock the doors quickly enough." A sad look came to her eyes, and he reached under her chin and lifted her face until she looked at him. "It's not that big a deal until it's a big deal."

He watched as the understanding whispered across her expression. His thumb gently stroked her chin, sliding up to her bottom lip, and he said in a low voice, "And I do want to spend more time with you."

He glanced around and confirmed they were alone. Grinning, he lowered his head and brushed his lips across hers.

Startled, she stepped back, her gaze widening. Her mouth opened, but no sound came out.

He chuckled. "I know. That surprised me too." He turned and walked away. "You stay safe."

He walked out the door, hopped into the truck, and said to Logan, "Okay, let's go." The truck didn't move. He turned to glance at Logan. "What's up?" He saw a silly grin on Logan's face. Narrowing his gaze, he asked suspiciously, "What?"

"Before we go, you might want to wipe the cherry-red lipstick off your lips."

Jace groaned. "Figures," he said in disgust.

He checked the glove box and found several small traveling packs of tissues. He pulled one out and wiped his lips. Sure enough cherry-red lipstick came away onto the white Kleenex. He stared at it and smiled.

Logan turned on the engine and pulled the truck from the parking spot. "Now the real question is, did you do that to further our business or because you couldn't help yourself?"

Jace snorted. "That doesn't deserve an answer."

Logan chuckled. "Wait 'til the guys hear about it."

"Or you could not say anything," Jace snapped. Then he shook his head. "You're trying to get on my nerves."

"I already got the answer, so it's no biggie."

Jace settled in as they headed to the city. "Where are you going now?"

"We have interviews with the men and women who were at the river rescue when the cousins drowned."

"Good. They're all together?"

"Yes, they're all training at their warehouse."

Logan took several turns, following the GPS instructions. They ended up outside a large warehouse with kayaks, canoes, and trailers parked to the side and then ATVs, motorbikes, and dirt bikes on the other.

Jace smiled. "You know? If I wasn't doing what I am now, I could see myself doing this."

"With all that adrenaline you carry, I don't think being a weekend warrior would be enough."

They walked inside to find they were expected.

"Good afternoon, gentlemen. I'm Troy Allroy. According to Ice, you need to speak with our team members."

"With whoever was at the river at the time of the two men's deaths."

Troy's face settled into somber lines. "Not everyone is here. John is holed up at home, still struggling with what happened. They were very knowledgeable men, some of our best. They were both instructors."

"Did you see what happened to them?"

Troy shook his head. "I had gone to the parking lot. We were trying to get the big trucks as close to the edge of the river to utilize the winches. The line on that truck is much longer than on the others."

"Did you take any pictures of the accident scene?"

"While it was all happening, no. There was no time."

"You know anybody who would have video or images from that afternoon?"

Troy frowned. "Maybe some of the crew did."

"That's one of the reasons we want to speak with every-body."

Jace asked, "How many TxSAR volunteers do you have in this area?"

"We try to keep twenty trained volunteers so we're fully staffed."

"But several have quit recently," Jace said.

"We had several drop out last year. We're always looking for more. I'm not sure you can ever have too many volun-teers. We don't pay them, yet we need them."

"Twenty doesn't sound like anywhere near enough."

Troy nodded. "After we lost the two men in the river, a lot of our new trainees walked away. It's all nice and glamor-ous until your life's on the line. The reality was a little bit too much for some of them. We get a rush of people wanting to help—around thirty to thirty-five—but, by the end of the training session, it boils down to about ten. And, of those ten, we will be lucky to have five happy to stay when reality sinks in, if you know what I mean."

"Yes, we know exactly what you mean." The military was like that too. Just because recruits were in the military and had been trained didn't mean they had that gift. Or that presence of mind to handle what was thrown at them.

Troy got down to business then. "I set aside one of the rooms for you. Amber and Amy are ready first for you to interview."

Jace and Logan nodded, and Troy led them to a nearby room.

Sitting down at the table with a notepad in hand, Jace brought out his phone. "I want to record the conversations, if that's okay with you," he said when the two women sat down. He glanced over at Amy. She was a tall, strapping woman in her mid-thirties.

Amber was stockier. She had shoulders like a linebacker. But she wasn't fat. She was one of those heavily muscled women; her tone was direct, her voice gentle. "I knew both Ronnie and Howard for years. I worked alongside them. I was trained under them. When we lost both in one event like that, it was a huge load on all of us," she said.

"Did you see what happened to them?"

She shook her head. "No, I didn't. But it was chaos. They were working the vehicle drowning the fastest, a truck with one man trapped inside. Bill, Peter, and Frank had the van in the river, trying to get a mother and several children out of it, and I was with another vehicle, trying to get a baby strapped in the back seat, and the water was rising. I only heard after the fact what happened."

"I agree with Amber," Amy said, then she frowned. "Also a lot of spectators were on the banks, watching. They wanted to help, but so often nobody knows what to do."

Jace and Logan asked several more questions and then thanked the two women.

Amy said, "The only reason you would be doing this is if you suspect either foul play or negligence. I can tell you this, they weren't negligent. They were highly skilled and knew what they were about." She turned and walked out, pausing outside the door. Amber waited for her.

The two exchanged a look.

"And I ask kindly that you don't say anything to slur these two men's names."

"That's not what we're here for," Jace said.

The door opened, and a man walked in. Twenty-eight-year-old Peter Cole sat down. He looked like a young

Viking. The minute they started asking questions, his voice turned husky, his eyes brightened with tears.

"I still miss them," he said. "Every day. They were mentors for the younger ones here. They had such a great camaraderie. They were cousins but could've been brothers. They were in fact best friends."

The next question was important, as it could set off a storm among everybody here. "Did they have any fights or any enemies within this group?"

Peter stared at him in shock. "No, absolutely not."

"Who went to help Ronnie when he first went under?"

"I didn't see who was there first. I only saw when Howard went after him. No," he quickly corrected himself, "I didn't see him then. I briefly saw him trying to help Ronnie."

"Did you see Howard go under?"

Peter shook his head. "A group tried to haul the two of them back to the riverbank again. But I know they were struggling. The water was questionable at that point. Debris was coming down the river, logs separating the rescuers, and I think they got caught in the debris and went under."

"Interesting." Jace jotted down a few notes. Debris hadn't come up yet in the other interviews. "Did you see the debris?"

Peter shook his head. "No, I think Troy might've said something to me about it. When I did see it, there were trees and people all over the place."

Jace nodded. "Good enough. What about the other rescuers?"

"There was so much chaos, nobody saw when Ronnie went under, and nobody saw Howard go under as he tried to help his cousin. Several mentioned debris, but nobody can say what it was or if it hit them. We were all busy doing our own thing."

Jace understood. But it wasn't helpful. After the interviews, all the volunteers reassembled into the room together, and he asked, "Do any of you know if bystanders took any videos?"

Peter nodded. "I do. Several of the local reporters were there, taking videos."

Jace and Logan gathered the rest of the information, thanked the crew, and headed back out again. "Wonder if we can get a tape from the media?" Jace asked as he hopped into the truck.

"Let's make the call now. It's only three o'clock. We might get in today to see them."

Logan made the phone call while Jace went over his notes. It still bothered him that nobody saw the two men go under. He didn't know what he was expecting. But it would've been nice if somebody had seen that moment when both men got into trouble.

Logan hung up the phone. "They're expecting us. Two reporters were down there. Both have videos of the nightmare. The media outlet didn't want to air them because the two men were both respected members of the community. They were afraid it would be considered in bad taste."

Excited they finally had something tangible to look at, they drove to the news station. Inside they met Henry.

He led them into his office and said, "I was down there with Andrew. We both had video cameras, but they've been uploaded to our servers, so I'll put them up and see if they're of any help to you."

He punched some keys on his computer and then pointed to a large screen behind them.

Jace and Logan walked closer as the video started to play. "The water level was massive." Jace whistled. "It's a wonder anybody survived this."

"I have to admit, I thought of that myself when I was standing on the bank, safe and sound," Henry said. "It was pretty scary at the time."

Several rescuers were in the water. All wore the proper safety harnesses, and many of the team were on shore, letting the lines out as needed. "The teams are supposed to work in pairs with a spotter keeping an eye on what's happening to one in the river." As Jace and Logan went through the film, they could see several rescuers they'd spoken to.

Henry said, "These are the two men who died. Both were rescuing a man trapped inside that truck. The angle and flow of the water made that the most difficult rescue. On the side you can see some of the team helping the woman and kids from the van."

As they watched, a team member helped a woman out of the van with a child in her arms, who was passed to another rescuer, followed by another child and another child. Jace's eyes wandered to one of the children. He forced himself to keep watch on the two men. Several other people still hung around on the riverbank.

Then one man went down, followed by another. It was confusing to tell the volunteers apart with the water threatening to push them underwater, but also because each TxSAR member wore helmets. With the choppy water, it was hard to confirm if they were in trouble. And that was strictly from watching the video feed. He couldn't imagine what the situation was like from the shore in the ugly weather. There didn't appear to be anybody else around them. "Can you stop that and play it back slowly?"

Obligingly Henry restarted the video a few frames back. This time they all watched carefully. Although people were milling about, trying to help both in and out of the water, nobody seemed to be near the cousins.

"Can we see the other film now please?" Logan asked.

They waited a few minutes for the feeds to change; then the second video came up. This was similar but from a slightly different angle. It didn't show much more though. It did reveal several others close by the cousins. Jace watched as the helmets bobbed and shifted. "I see a third man there."

Henry stepped forward and studied it. "There is a third man, I think," he said in surprise. "I never saw him before."

"And yet we have all the TxSAR men fully accounted for."

Logan tapped the screen, gently circling where all the other rescuers were working. "I'm counting the four we spoke to today, plus Frank and Bill who weren't at the center. But there's an extra. Troy was in the parking lot." He turned to look at Henry and said, "Did you see Troy in the parking lot?"

Henry frowned. "I think so. It's John you're missing. He was there that day too."

Chapter 8

B Y TWO O'CLOCK, Emily was ready to leave her office again. With the head office's decision and the news from Jace and Logan, she was feeling hemmed in. Not to mention the cases stacked up high on both sides of her desk. She needed a distraction, but she also needed to move forward. Considering she had to contact Lyle's wife, who was the same woman she'd caught in bed with her fiancé, she'd do a lot to push that phone call off. As she sat staring, the phone rang. It was the receptionist. "I have a Sicily Ranger Cowichan on the phone. She needs to talk to the insurance agent on her husband's life insurance policy. I looked it up in the records, and that's you."

"I'm not the agent on record, but it's been deferred to me as it's connected to several other cases," Emily said. "Put her through."

When Sicily came on the line, Emily introduced herself formally, then said, "What can I help you with?"

"My husband had an insurance policy, and he was killed in a hit-and-run a few days ago. What is happening? And why I haven't gotten the money?"

Emily listened intently, looking for clues in Sicily's voice. And although there was a slight hitch to her tone when saying her husband had been in a hit-and-run a few days ago, no grief or anything resembling sorrow was in her voice. "We are aware of the policy, and our investigation is in progress," Emily said. "What can you tell me about your husband's death?"

Sicily was hesitant at first but gained strength when she answered, "The police have all the details. Basically we were having a barbecue at our house with several friends, and an ex-boyfriend—who we have a restraining order against—came to the party and started a fight. After he left, my husband laughed and went inside to calm down so he could return to the party and we could change the atmosphere from being upsetting." She paused for a moment, then continued. "He didn't come back out, and I think it was about an hour later, I went looking for him. There was no sign of him in the house. When I told the guests to spread out and look for him, we found him out on the street, where he'd been run over."

At this point, her voice dropped, and the hitch became more pronounced. "We called the police and the ambulance, but there was no saving him."

"And your ex-boyfriend, what happened to him?"

Sicily's voice clipped off. "I don't know, and I don't care."

"Right," Emily said in a dry tone, realizing, if Sicily did know, she wasn't telling. "I'm taking down notes. I'll contact the police to get a copy of their report as well. I also need to study the autopsy report to make sure everything is in line."

"Then get it," Sicily said, her tone irate. "What does any of that have to do with the insurance policy?"

"Because we don't pay out in certain instances," Emily said in a neutral tone. "So, until we've completed our investigation, I can't write you a check."

"Oh, please take care of that as soon as possible. I need

the money to pay off my mortgage."

And Sicily hung up.

Emily stared down at the phone and said quietly, "I bet you do." But just because she didn't like the woman and didn't like what the woman had done to her, that was no reason to believe she had anything to do with Lyle's death. In which case she would likely rake in one million dollars. Unless Emily could prove Sicily had a hand in her husband's death.

As much as Emily hated the idea of that woman getting the money, she had to have proper grounds for denying the claim. And, although insurance companies found ways to not step up and pay out money, very few viable reasons to do so existed in the life insurance field. As she stared at the phone, she realized she had yet another reason why she couldn't step out of the office. Because, with Sicily having called Emily, she had no excuse to see Sicily now.

This really was a case of wait and see. And sometimes these things didn't happen quickly.

Hearing heavy footsteps coming her way, she peered around the corner of her cubicle to see Wilson walking toward her.

When he got to her side, he leaned down and said, "The head office is strict on their stance."

She grimaced. "Okay. If they are, they are."

He patted her on the shoulder. "If they give you a hard time, you can send them to me."

She nodded at him. "You're a bigger pushover than I am."

Wilson shook his head. "Not when it comes to company money. I want a job for the next fifteen to twenty years, so I'll not be handing out information that will get me fired."

She smiled and watched him walk away.

She opened her email program and, with a cc to Wilson, sent Ice an email stating the company line on the information from the database.

After she hit Send, she shrugged it off. It wasn't her problem. She knew perfectly well Ice would contact Wilson and potentially go above him. It was up to Ice to make that decision. As soon as Emily got instructions that she could hand over the information, then she would. Until then she could only hope Ice managed to do what Emily couldn't.

When her phone rang the next time, she picked up the receiver to hear US West Wind Life Insurance was calling. She dealt with other insurance companies all the time. In this case, it was James. "Hey, James, how are you doing?"

"I was doing okay until I looked into the death of one of our policy holders. When I checked, I found out from the detective that your case and my case are linked."

She sat back in her chair. "Who's the owner of the policy? Who are we talking about here?"

"Richard Manton. Apparently he was drowned in his car?" James's voice rose at the end in disbelief.

She knew how he felt. "Ouch."

"You know what I'm talking about?"

"Yes. He went to a family barbecue to see a woman and her husband, even though a restraining order had been issued against him for said woman and husband. The husband and your guy got into a fight. Apparently when the fight was finally broken up, your Manton left, and the husband went into the house to calm down."

"How did that work out for him?" James said drily.

"It didn't. This is where it gets odd. He didn't show back up at his barbecue, so his wife went looking for him, and they found him in the street where he'd been run over."

"The same street where my guy was found drowned?"

"Yes, about fifty yards away from each other."

"And do you have any idea what's going on?"

"No. The police investigation is ongoing, and I don't think anybody has any idea what happened yet. I have a copy of the autopsy but haven't had a chance to study it."

James continued. "The assumption at the moment is that Richard Manton died by having a funnel jammed down his throat and water poured into his lungs. There was also water in his stomach."

"Of course. I mean, surely there is an easier way to kill somebody."

"He would've been unconscious at the time," James said. "So we're definitely talking murder."

"Right. I'm waiting for the police investigation to conclude to make sure that the beneficiary, who in my case is Lyle Cowichan's wife, Sicily, is not involved in his murder."

"Now that's interesting because the life insurance beneficiary in my case," James said very softly, "is his ex-girlfriend, Sicily Ranger Cowichan. So she potentially stands to gain from both their deaths."

"Wow." Emily shook her head. "That definitely confuses the issue."

"A notable confusion, considering she's about to benefit from two deaths, one her husband, the other her ex-boyfriend. I wonder if she has a replacement standing in line."

Emily winced. "I drove past the property, taking a look at the crime scene yesterday, and a white SUV was in the driveway."

"Have you run the plates yet?"

"Yes. A thirty-four year-old accountant named Jimmy Burton. Divorced a year ago, no known attachments."

"Does he have a life insurance policy?" James asked. "Because if he does, he better run."

"I'm checking my database right now. Have you got a policy on him?"

The two ran through their databases looking for the potential boyfriend.

"I admit I'm happy to say that I don't have a policy on him," Emily said.

James said thoughtfully, "Neither do we. But I think we should point the police in that direction to see if they can find out about a policy with another company."

"Right. It's definitely something to be followed up on."

After she hung up, she called Ice. "Sorry about the company line," she said immediately.

Ice laughed. "Bureaucracy at it's best. I know and understand. I'm already working on it, so not to worry."

Emily grinned. "I figured you might have a few more tricks up your sleeve."

"Did you have some other reason for calling?"

"Yes. When I drove past Sicily's house, a white SUV was parked in the drive." She rattled off the plate number and the related info, plus how she saw the driver of the SUV kissing Sicily. "So I'm wondering, as her husband and ex-boyfriend are now dead, is this Burton guy a potential waiting-in-the-wings partner? And since Sicily stands to gain from both deaths, I was thinking the police need to know and find out if Burton has a life insurance policy."

Ice whistled. "Wouldn't that be something?"

Emily stared off in the distance. "I know what she did to me. At the time I was pretty damn angry."

Ice's voice turned brisk. "Let's hope Lyle was happily married."

"Amen to that."

After she hung up, Emily updated her notes. She took a look at the list of names Ice had sent. She realized that the TxSAR Center was on her route home. She didn't want to double up on the investigation, but she hadn't heard back from Jace and Logan. She wondered if she should stop by the center and take a look. She picked up the phone and called the center, explained who she was and that she needed to speak to several of the members.

A man named Troy said, "We've already had two men here interviewing everybody. What's going on?"

Keeping her voice neutral, she said, "This is a standard procedure. Several insurance policies are involved that we must investigate before we write the checks."

"Most of our members have gone home. Maybe you can talk to the two investigators who were here earlier today." He rattled off two names that she knew very well: Jace Colley and Logan Redding.

"I'll talk to them first. If I have any further questions, I'll get back to you."

"Thanks. We're pretty busy here right now," Troy said with relief in his voice. "It's very unsettling to still have these deaths being investigated weeks later. We're like a family. We need to heal and move on."

"Speaking of which, you lost a member a year or so ago?"

"Yes. And now since then we lost four more members, and our numbers have been decimated. And we're trying hard to bring in more volunteers. We're well into hurricane season, and flooding will be an issue no matter what the area."

"Thanks." She hung up and studied the phone in her hand. She couldn't imagine trying to get volunteers to step up to help in natural disasters after losing two of their own men in a rescue. Still, volunteers were a vital force for emergency disaster relief the world over. Some people liked that sense of adventure and living on the edge, but so many others wanted to make sure that, even though they were willing to help anyone in trouble, they themselves would be as safe as possible.

She brought up the TxSAR website. On the front page was a memorial to the two cousins. Not the two who were murdered in town, but the two who had drowned. That was appropriate. They had both died while helping others. She read on about the organization and the people involved. Troy was now running the center. She searched for various members, trying to come up with any tidbits of names and places, citations, medals, etc. But there was scant information. Ronnie and Howard had been at the top of the organization. Ronnie, the leader, and Howard, his backup.

Before that, Ken Foster had run the center for close to a decade and had earned a lot of respect in that time. His death had been keenly felt. She couldn't imagine having to deal with the fallout of losing those who managed the center.

She shut down her computer, picked up some of the files she wanted to go over at home, stored them in her briefcase, and locked up. As she walked out of the building, several people called out to say goodbye. She waved and stepped out into the afternoon sun.

She was still unsettled by so much going on in her personal life. She'd missed the funeral of the two cousins, and maybe that was the way it should be. Though one had been her husband for a short time, that didn't mean she'd be welcome at the funeral. That wasn't to say she couldn't go to the cemetery and say goodbye. She knew the family had plots out by the Blanco River. It was on a high point off to the side of the old cemetery. The family plots had been there for generations.

Making a fast decision, she changed lanes and drove toward the cemetery. When she had been married to Ronnie, the two had bought a double plot. After their divorce, she'd left it with him. It was his family's burial area, and she had no idea what part of the country she would end up in. But, in his case, she knew exactly where he would end up. And he was happy with that. She'd struggled with the double-plot concept, found it creepy. He'd found it comforting.

She drove into the gates, making her way around the curvy road. She could see multiple monuments and flat stones all around since the cemetery had been in use for a couple hundred years.

She drove up to the main parking lot and stopped. She took a moment to reorient herself as to where she was; then she walked to the closest path and headed off in the direction of the plot. She hadn't been here in a long time. But it wasn't something you forgot easily. At the area she thought was correct, she could see two monuments covered in flowers, and she realized she'd found the cousins. She stood in front and read the names and the dates. With her hands in her pockets, she thought about all they had been to her.

She'd married one, gone out with the other. They were both damned good men. She shook her head, even now feeling the tears in the back of her eyes.

She glanced around the area, wondering if Lyle would be here too. He'd been as much a family man as the others. But she didn't know if all the cousins had plots here too. She wandered through the nearby markers, reading the names and the dates, finding a sense of peace in the continuity. With a last long look at the grave markers, she finally, with the wind starting to bite, turned and headed back to her car.

A woman walked toward her. She stopped and asked, "Did you know my husband?"

Emily frowned. "Who was your husband?"

"Ronnie Williamson."

Emily gave her a ghost of a smile. "I don't know that you want to hear this, but I was his first wife."

Surprise lit the woman's face. She held out her hand and said, "I'm Rose. Ronnie and I were married for six years. He did mention you, but I never heard the details."

Emily smiled and put her hand back in her pocket. "Not a whole lot to say. We were high school sweethearts, married young, and didn't have a clue what we're getting ourselves into. We divorced almost as quickly."

Rose nodded toward the monuments. "And yet you're here?"

Emily nodded. "I was raised with the family close by. He will always have a part of my heart. Just because we divorced doesn't mean I didn't care." She was surprised at the understanding on Rose's face.

"I'm glad," she said simply. "I'm glad he knew you. He was a wonderful man."

Emily smiled. "I'm glad he found you and married again. That he was happy right to the end."

With understanding, the two women continued, each on their individual paths. Emily headed back to her car and Rose to her husband's grave where she stood for however long. She was still there when Emily pulled her car out of the parking lot and headed home.

Tears were in her eyes, a sense of loss in her heart, with grief still rippling through her. But there was also peace. Peace he'd been blessed to have Rose. Pleased he'd gone on to live a full, rich life and that he'd been respected. That he'd been a man others looked up to.

There was a whole lot worse people could say as an epitaph.

ARMED WITH A copy of the two news videos, Jace and Logan retraced their steps to the TxSAR Center. With the members once again together in one room, Jace brought up the video. They were a somber group, watching the last moments of Ronnie's and Howard's lives. When the third man was visible, Jace stopped the video and pointed at the screen. "Does anybody know who that is?"

Everyone shook their heads.

Jace said, "Every one of you said they were alone when they went under. But this shows a third person. Does anybody know who it could be?"

Peter said, "It could be anybody. There was so much chaos—the river's flowing, people screaming and yelling and panicking inside their vehicles, trying to get free. There was a dog barking like crazy. There were people in the water, on the shore. Some helping. Some hindering. And then, above it all, there was the storm, pelting us with rain, blinding us at times, hindering our vision at other times."

Jace nodded and in a gentle voice said, "We're not accusing any of you of anything. We're trying to identify this person."

"Yeah, we'd like to know what the hell's going on here

too," said one of the older men, a sullen look on his face.

Jace studied him. "We're not accusing anyone of anything."

"Good. Because we've been doing these rescues for decades. We've hardly lost anybody."

"That's not right," Peter said. "Last year we lost Ken Foster. He ran the center."

"Yeah, that was another freak accident. So is this."

"Is that so?" Jace said. "Then we need to figure out what happened. And let's not forget we've been hired by the TxSAR association to get to the bottom of this."

"Why is that anyway?" Troy asked belligerently. "You're not the police. They didn't even ask us all these questions."

"And that's sad," Logan said. "I guess the police are super busy, and this isn't a big concern for them. But wouldn't it be nice, if you had been the one who died, that somebody checked to make sure all was okay? And that it doesn't happen to anyone else?"

"Are you thinking the equipment failed? That we didn't do our job? Because you're way off base there," Troy snapped. "You won't make us a case study to improve on next time."

"We're not here to make an example of what not to do. But we must follow our mandate as well," Jace said. "Why don't you start by telling us what happens when you get a call."

Troy continued. "When we get a call, depending on the details as to how bad the scenario is, we make the determination whether to go or not. Given that we have a small team, we usually need everyone available. In this case we had four vehicles in the water and an unknown number of people to rescue, and it was a case of whoever was available should drop everything and run to the river."

"Did you have any warning?" Logan asked.

Peter shook his head. "We knew the floodwaters were rising, but we hadn't heard the bridge was in any trouble. But it was an old bridge and was in need of repair. Then vehicles slammed into the guardrail and went over into the river."

"Yes, I'm sure police accident reports about it are somewhere," Troy said with a dismissive wave of his hand.

"Yes, probably," Jace said. "Like a lot of reports, they're often very scanty."

"There isn't anything to say," Troy protested. "We went out. We did our job, and two of our men lost their lives."

Amber started to sniffle.

"I presume you all knew Ronnie?"

"Ronnie had been running the center since Ken Foster passed away last year," Peter said.

"How was he as a manager?" Logan asked, standing, his legs slightly spread apart, his arms crossed over his chest. His posture wasn't intended to be intimidating, but it was a no-nonsense stance. *I'm here until doomsday, until I get the answers to my questions.* And the crowd understood.

"He was great. He was knowledgeable and very fair," Peter said.

"If Ken hadn't died last year, we would still have him as a manager because he was also great. We were lucky to have had such competent and skilled men here," Amber said, teary-eyed still.

Jace nodded. "A lot of qualities go into making a leader. And, in this kind of work, you have to handle almost anything."

"In situations like this, we get everything thrown at us.

We don't know if we'll chop down trees or if we need longer ropes," Peter said. "We're forever coming up with new scenarios to plan for."

Peter turned to Troy. "You had to get the truck from the parking lot, for the longer ropes, right?"

Troy nodded.

"The two trucks we had parked nearest the river had winches and lines, but they weren't long enough. Troy was moving the bigger unit over while all we could do was watch as the bank flooded away. There was barely any place for us to stand, short of hanging onto the rope ourselves. And that is a recipe for disaster. You can hang onto a man's weight easy enough on solid ground when the weather cooperates, but, once your feet start to slide or the man is pulled in by the current, then you're pulled in too."

"Were Ronnie and Howard on the same line?" Logan asked.

"No. That's not how we operate if we can avoid it. In that instance, they went out on separate lines."

"There was some slack. When the trapped man was free of his truck, Ronnie hooked him onto his line, and we started to bring him in. I presumed Ronnie was secured to something else … or someone else at that point," Amber said.

Amy nodded. "Ronnie and Howard were working on the truck with a single male inside. I was working on getting the woman and the man out of the fourth vehicle in the river, and they had their dog too."

Jace listened, getting a good feel for what happened and when the call went out. He understood they could only recall so much because the action happened quickly.

"At one point I looked around, and there appeared to be

dozens of bystanders—media, police, and citizen volunteers," Peter said. "It was chaos."

"Who was the last person to be rescued?"

"That was the man from the vehicle Ronnie was working on," Amber said.

"And that'll be the man's head you were trying to identify in the video," Troy said, pointing to the still shot on the wall before them.

"What was holding Ronnie and Howard together? Or was the rescued man hooked to a new line?"

"All three men should have had separate lines, but, if there was a problem, they could have hooked together or onto something else temporarily. The rope holding Ronnie was tattered when we pulled it in from the river. Like it had been cut by a sharp piece of metal from the vehicle. We assumed that's how they ended up downriver. Alternatively they could have been swept away while they tried to change their security line."

"The rescued man was on his own line. I was there, holding him up. You guys pulled both of us out," Troy said in triumph, as if happy he could finally remember.

Amy in relief said, "That's right. We dragged both of you out of that river, didn't we?"

"Damn good thing you did. That current was battering us against the vehicles hard."

"Okay, so now we have Ronnie and his cousin working at the vehicle. Who had their lines?"

Peter said, "I did."

Everybody turned to look at him.

"You had both lines?" Jace asked.

Peter shook his head. "I had Ronnie's. From the beginning we had his line secured to one of the trucks. When

Howard went in, we secured him to the same truck too, but I was watching the lines, making sure they were free of debris and that I could yank them in fast. And to send messages."

At Jace's questioning look, Peter explained further. "When men are caught up in something like that, the line is too far out to communicate with words, especially over the roar of the river current and the additional noise of the rainstorm. We use the ropes and pull on them in order to get their attention."

Both Logan and Jace nodded. Jace said, "We've both had similar situations in the military."

Peter nodded with relief. "We're supposed to use all kinds of hand signals, but honestly it's damn hard to do at times like that. With the switch in the trucks, we hooked up Ronnie's and Howard's lines to the new truck, and I moved down to help carry the kids to the ambulances waiting off to the side. But the weather was deadly. And we've done this many times, so there wasn't any reason to think something had gone wrong. At least not right away."

"That's another good point," Logan said. "You said the storm was raging?"

"The rain was coming down heavily." Peter pointed to the video. "That looks gray, but, in truth, it was streaming water. Sometimes we could see, and sometimes there was no clarity at all."

Logan pulled his cell phone free of the USB connector to the camera that played the media video. "That makes sense." He could feel the almost palpable release of tension in the room when he turned back to the others. "If you think of anything else"—he pulled out their cards and handed them out—"please call us and let us know." When he came to Troy, he asked, "How many are in the unit now?"

"There were fourteen. Now we're down to ten. We've got fourteen new trainees up and coming."

"And how many of those new trainees were at that rescue?" Logan asked.

Troy shook his head. "None. I don't think they were called in. That would have been Ronnie and Howard's decision."

"So, of those at the river that day, how many do I still have to speak to?"

Everyone looked at each other.

"I guess three. John, Bill, and Frank."

"We need their contact information. We must interview them, same as anybody else in here."

He stared at Troy for a long moment, then glanced around at the others.

Amy said, "Give them the list, Troy. Let's make sure we do right by the men we lost. As they would've done right by us."

Troy waited a moment, gave a clipped nod, and turned to walk into the office.

Amy snorted. "We could sure use Ronnie as our leader now. We're all lost without him."

"In normal circumstances, if you had lost only one man, who would've been the next leader and manager of this unit?" Logan asked.

The response was instant. "Howard would've been the next in line as manager. No way would anybody else have been."

"They were both that good?"

Everyone nodded.

"They were damn great," Peter said.

The others nodded once again.

"Now that Ronnie and Howard are gone, who's next in line?" Jace asked.

"John," multiple people said in unison.

"How does management change here?" Logan asked.

The volunteers all looked at each other and shrugged. "Unfortunately here lately it's been through death."

Jace winced. "That's a hard way to get promoted."

"It sure is."

Then Troy returned with a piece of paper. He held it out and said, "Here is the information on the three men." He'd marked them with an asterisk. "Bill and Frank are likely to be at the center any time. John, well, I don't know what's happening with him."

Jace smiled. "I appreciate that, thank you. Remember, everyone. If you find or think of anything important, give us a shout. Other than that, thank you very much. You've been very helpful."

He turned and walked away. He knew the volunteers were of the opinion that the two men had died in a freak accident. It was terrible, but there was nothing anyone could do. But Jace also knew that the volunteers hadn't seen what he and Logan had seen. Of course the other video had been a hands-only shot of the third guy. He hadn't seen it at first either on the second video as the angle was confusing. Only a corner was showing, but the third man had a helmet on, and that meant he was one of the rescuers. And that brought them to another discussion. He turned and looked back. Everyone was standing around, talking. He knew he'd upset them by asking questions.

Jace called out, "Excuse me." He took several steps toward them. Weariness settled on their faces again. "What happened to the equipment the men wore when they were pulled out of the river?"

Troy frowned. "I brought the safety harnesses back in the truck. The ropes were cut at the end, so I had to recut and rebind the end so we could reuse them."

"Okay, that makes sense." Jace again glanced one more time at every face, gauging their reactions. "And their helmets? Did you get those back too?"

Troy frowned and looked at the others. They all looked at each other and shrugged. He shook his head. "No. I didn't get either of those back," he said. "Maybe the police still have them. Maybe the river ate them. For all I know, maybe the family kept them as a memento of a fallen soldier."

"I like that." Jace lifted a hand in goodbye and walked away.

Logan looked at him when he reached the truck. "What was that all about?"

"I might have a very good idea of how those men died and by whose hand. What I don't know is why. And I can't prove any of it," he said simply.

Logan whistled. "If you think you know that much, you're way ahead of the game." He opened the driver's door and hopped in.

Jace walked around to the far side and got in the passenger seat. As he was about to resume their conversation, Logan's phone rang.

He pulled it out and took a look at the ID. "What's up, Ice?" He paused only a moment. "We're heading to the hotel right now. We've finished interviewing all but the last three volunteers and watching the two videos from one of the media outlets." He listened again. "Why?"

Logan listened while Jace watched. He couldn't hear the other end of the conversation, but Logan checked his watch.

"We still need several hours here, possibly a day or so. How many men do you need on this job?" He glanced at Jace. "One of us can return while the other stays, but we only have one set of wheels."

Jace's eyebrows rose.

"Sure, we can do that. I don't think Jace would mind staying an extra night."

Inside Jace smiled. If he was staying an extra night, he hoped to ask out a certain lady for dinner.

When Logan hung up the phone, he faced Jace. "Another job has come in. It's a top priority. Stone and Merk, likely Rhodes, are going too."

"Where and when?"

"I have to head to Houston. Ice will call us back when she has a flight booked for me." Logan turned on the engine and started to drive away. "Are you okay staying in Austin alone?"

Jace nodded. "I am."

Logan grinned. "You're probably delighted because I highly doubt you'll be alone tonight."

Jace smiled. "Oh, as much as I'd like to think that I could work that fast, I don't think it'll happen. However, dinner is certainly possible."

"Remember that Levi expects the job to get done too."

Jace nodded. "I don't have a problem with that."

Logan's phone rang again before he got a chance to pull out to the main road. Grabbing the GPS, Jace punched in the address for the small airfield as Logan repeated it to him, so they could get there as fast as possible. Luckily they appeared to be nearby.

As Logan tossed the phone down beside him, he said, "Typical Ice. When things need to happen, she makes them happen now."

"We'll be at the airport in fifteen minutes."

"I need to make it in ten as that damn flight will leave in twenty."

The drive passed in a blur. Neither man spoke as Logan wove through the traffic. Thankfully rush hour was long gone, but the day was turning to dusk, making it hard to see. The GPS cranked out instructions, which he followed.

They raced into the parking lot, and Ice called again. Logan grabbed his phone. "We just arrived." He slammed the truck door, tossed the keys to Jace. "I'm gone. See if you can lock down this investigation before I get back." He gave Jace a big grin and a wave, and then he bolted.

Jace hopped from the truck and walked around to the driver's side. He watched as Logan jogged across the tarmac to a small plane off to the side. The propellers were already turning. Somebody stood at the top of the stairs to lead him in. Logan yelled and waved. Jace snorted as he watched Logan disappear inside the plane. The stairs were lifted, and within seconds the plane took off.

He had to admit Logan was right. When Ice wanted something done, dammit, she got it done.

With the keys in hand he sat inside the truck, pulled out his phone, and dialed Emily's number. When she answered, he said, "Logan had to leave. I'm staying in Austin for the night, maybe two, depending on how quickly I get this wrapped up. I'd like to take you out to dinner. If you're interested."

Chapter 9

EMILY STEPPED FROM her car, her phone to her ear. "I just got home. I went out to the cemetery in an effort to find some peace for the two men I've lost."

"In that case, how about a bottle of red wine and some Italian food?" Jace asked.

She chuckled. "You mean, because Curry House was one choice, so we have to have the other?"

"I'm good with pizza on a riverbank somewhere with a bottle of wine. But I'm not sure I want to be anywhere that reminds me of the case. It might be nice to take a few minutes away from reality."

"Well, if you bring the wine, I could make dinner."

"Done," he said instantly. "I hate being in a hotel room by myself."

She laughed. "I need a little time to shower and start something for dinner."

"Tell me when you want me there."

She smiled at the gentleness in his voice. "It's almost like you prefer this over a restaurant," she teased.

"I do. Home-cooked food? I'd take that any day."

She laughed. "What if I'm a terrible cook?"

"I doubt it, but that would be okay too because you're a beautiful woman, so, if I get to sit across the table and just smile at you, I'm fine."

At that she laughed out loud. "None of that flattery, please. If you pick up a bottle of wine, I'll see you at my place in, say, forty minutes?"

"You got it."

She hung up, a silly grin on her face. She walked through the underground parking lot and took the elevator to the fourth floor. Inside her apartment, she had a shower and got changed.

Her mind buzzed about what she could possibly cook. He'd been planning to take her out for Italian, and she had passed. The question was, what did she have to cook? In the fridge she found spinach, pesto that was a couple days old, and some chicken. She put on a pot of water for the pasta and started the sauce. She cut the chicken into small pieces. When the pasta was almost done, the chicken was sautéing in a creamy pesto sauce.

He still hadn't arrived, so she got to work on a salad. As she cleaned up, her doorbell rang. She turned the heat down on the sauce and realized the pasta needed another moment. She headed to the front door, calling out, "Coming."

She opened the door and smiled when he handed her pink roses. "Oh, wow. These are beautiful," she said with a bright smile. "Thank you so much. I can't tell you the last time anybody brought me flowers."

"Good. I was afraid every man did this for you."

She snorted. "Some have, but the best customs have gone by the wayside." She smiled back at him, adding, "Bringing fresh flowers will never get old for me. Come on in, and make yourself at home. Dinner is almost ready."

He took off his jacket and draped it on the back of a chair. She brought out a vase, trimmed the stems of the roses, and put them in, adding water, spreading them out slightly.

"It smells delicious," he commented. "And I wasn't kidding when I said I'd prefer a home-cooked meal over a restaurant any day."

"I like restaurants just fine. They give me a break from cooking. I live alone, so it's nice to have somebody to cook for. Cooking for yourself isn't the same."

"Well, anytime you want to cook a meal for me, you got it."

"Even if I cook a meal, Houston is a little far for you to come for dinner."

He gave her a long, slow, smoky smile.

She blinked, and sudden heat flared through her. "Now that smile is lethal," she complained when she could find her voice. "Tone it down."

"Why? Anytime you call, offering me dinner, I'll make the drive," he said seriously.

She gave him a startled look, saw the truth in his gaze, and blushed. "Well, that's nice to hear. But, if you come that far, you should stay for a couple days."

That smile dawned again.

She shook her head. And took a deep breath. "Wow."

"A couple days, like a weekend?"

And instantly she saw how this could possibly work. "I don't know that long-distance relationships turn out very well."

"I travel a lot anyway," he said. "Not everybody is happy with that."

"It wouldn't scare me off. I often work late. And, if I don't have something else to do, I have a tendency to work on weekends too."

"Well, having company would stop that."

"True enough. You live at the compound, don't you?"

He nodded. "It's a beautiful place, as you saw when you were there. Besides, if I came here for a weekend, no reason you can't visit me the next weekend."

"How about we step back a little and see how our evening goes?" she said drily. "I'm not exactly ready to jump into weekends at each other's places."

He chuckled. "I'll hold out hope for when you say yes."

She rolled her eyes at him and quickly served his plate.

He stood with a bottle of wine in his hand. "Do you have a corkscrew?"

She pointed to a drawer. He found it, took the cork out, and, at her direction, found two wineglasses. When he poured each half full, she had their plates served with salad already on the table. He quickly hit a dimmer switch, turning off the kitchen lights, creating a nice atmosphere over the table.

As she sat down, she marveled, "This is a beautiful romantic dinner." Her smile deepened. "Thanks for inviting me out."

"Thanks for inviting me here instead." He lifted his glass and held it up. "To more romantic dinners."

She'd known he would be lethal. But she hadn't realized just how lethal. When he was with Logan, it had been easy to hold back her attraction. But now he was here, alone with her, in such an intimate setting. Well …

She took a deep breath and tried to push away the heat. She cast her mind around, looking for a topic that could be safely neutral. "How's the investigation going?"

"It's going," he said cheerfully. "I have to interview three more members we missed at the TxSAR Center. I tried to connect with them earlier but could only leave messages."

"And after that, what?"

"I still haven't met the wives yet. I'd love to talk with Jimmy Burton too if I get time."

She dropped her gaze and winced. "Oh, him."

"Yeah. The police are running a check to see if he has a life insurance policy."

She sucked in her breath at that. "Good. Do you think the four cases are related?"

"I'm not exactly sure yet. But I'm a whole lot closer to having a working hypothesis."

She looked at him hopefully. "Care to share?"

"Not yet. I have a pretty good line to tug though. Tomorrow, once I start tugging for real, I'm hoping to make the whole thing unravel."

She settled back. "I'm almost scared to ask."

"It doesn't matter if you do or not," he said, lifting a forkful of pasta to his mouth. "Until I get it settled, I won't tell you."

"You don't want to jinx it?"

He stared at her and answered slowly, "No. But, if I'm right, somebody has murdered five men. Maybe more. What I don't want to do is put you in danger. If I tell you anything, it's quite possible you'll get caught up in the middle."

She put down her fork, her stomach suddenly sick. "Are you serious? *Five* people could've been killed by the same hand?"

"I'm afraid it could be more," he said. He lifted his glass again. "How about we drink to it not being even that many?"

Taking it as a sign he was done with this difficult subject, she lifted her glass to his. "That much I'll drink to. But surely we have something better to toast than hoping the murderer didn't have so many victims."

He chuckled, his gaze warm and sexy. "Then how about we drink to us?"

She didn't even know how the conversation, the mood, the atmosphere had become so charged.

What was it about a warm room, a hot meal, a bottle of wine, and a sexy man to make her heart race? Okay, maybe not with *any* man. Something about being in the quiet comfort of his presence was like finding solace in being close to him.

"Heavy thoughts?"

She looked up, startled, then smiled. "If you only knew."

That steady gaze appeared to search deep into her eyes.

She stared back openly.

"I'd like to know."

She tilted her head to the side and contemplated him. "But would you really?"

He put down his fork, picked up his glass of wine, and took a sip. "I think one of the biggest problems with relationships is lack of communication," he said with a smile. "Right now it feels to me like you're considering us. Or me for that matter. And, if that's the truth, then I would really like to know what you think."

She let out her breath, slow and gentle. "You're right. I was thinking about you. Wondering how we got to this place so quickly."

His smile peeked out to match the grin in his eyes. "Tell me more," he teased.

She chuckled gently. "I was just thinking that, when I'm around you, I don't feel so flustered. I don't feel so stressed." She gazed at the wine swirling in her glass. "I can't explain it, but it's almost like a sense of peace when I'm with you. Your energy is very calm, very considerate. You don't go rushing around from job to job. You don't fly off the handle or appear to get stressed out over anything. In fact, you're very ... laid-back," she said lamely. "I know that's not quite the right word, but to say that you're very grounded doesn't sound right either."

He nodded his head. "I've heard things like reserved, boring. ... How about introverted?"

She shook her head, her gaze aligning with his. "No. That's not what I mean. The word I was thinking was *soulful.* As in, being around you gives me a sense of peace."

A warm light shone in his gaze. "Now that," he said, "is something I'd get behind."

She leaned back and watched as he finished his dinner. She was enjoying hers too, but watching him made her feel good. "Look at the way you're eating," she said. "Everything you do is easy. It's measured. It's careful, but it's not restrained. Every movement you make is with power and confidence. That is extremely attractive."

"You keep surprising me," he said. "Most of the time that's not the response I get."

"No?" she mused. "I can see that. For the wrong woman, you would probably come across as boring. Or maybe too determined to jump into something." She smiled when he dropped his gaze and continued to eat. "But that's not really the truth. I think, when you want to make a move, you do so very quickly. The same as you don't waste time with useless conversation. When you have something to say, you say it. And I think most of your actions are that way as well. You think things out way in advance, and, when it's time, you know exactly what moves to take."

"Not always," he said. "Lots of times life throws you a

curveball, and I don't know what I'm supposed to do with it."

She nodded. "I think that happens to all of us. But I think you catch those curveballs more often than not. For me, they land beside me and roll one way. When I try to pick them up, I realize, while I was dashing, it has already reversed its path.

"Even when you walk," she said, "it's very relaxed, loose-limbed, but every step you take is with confidence, as if you know exactly where you're going at all times."

He chuckled. "All of that sounds very flattering, but I don't want you getting the wrong impression of me. Even though I have a lot of military training, I made mistakes lots of times. We try very hard to train seamen well so they don't make mistakes. And I was a SEAL, so my training was more extensive. I knew mistakes could kill us when out on missions. So as a way to compensate for not making a mistake and getting us all killed, I would go through the plans over and over and over in my head. I would plan out every step I needed to take for every contingency I could imagine. I didn't want to be the one who would bring down my own crew. My unit, they are like brothers to me. And I couldn't possibly live with the guilt if I'd been responsible for any of them getting hurt."

She smiled. "Now that is what I mean. I can see that exactly—dedicated, honorable." He frowned at her, and she added, "Hero material all the way."

At that he laughed. "Better not let Levi hear you say that. I'm only just learning the pitfalls of that word myself."

She raised her eyebrows. "Now *that* you have to ex-plain."

She listened in fascination as she heard about the other

members of Legendary Security and how the women ended up finding a hero of their own and moving into the compound. "Of course not everybody has moved in. Anna and Flynn have an animal shelter just outside the compound. Michael bought property next door to the compound, is building a home there, and he'll be moving there with Mercy. Alina works at the hospital in Houston." He shrugged. "But they're all such a big family. And I like that."

"You miss the military, don't you?"

Once again he raised his gaze to look at her. That same direct look. As if he had nothing to hide.

And she believed it. That gaze had at its very core something so forthcoming and calm, so peaceful. She gave a happy sigh. "I can see you do. A resettling, a reshuffling of your life."

He gave a bark of laughter. "If you can see all that, I'm not doing a very good job. But you're right, I do miss the military. I was very close with my team members. All of us walked after our commander took a hit. He got blamed for doing something he wasn't supposed to. When the person who got him into trouble was bumped up to his place, and we had to take orders from him ..." Jace shook his head. "It was more than we could stomach."

"So all six of you walked away?"

He gave her a lopsided grin. "Yeah, and three of us—Michael, Tyson, and now me—are at Legendary Security. And Rory, Brandon and Liam work elsewhere." His grin widened. "At least for the moment."

She chuckled. "Levi's no fool."

"Neither is Ice," Jace said.

She smiled. "Very true. Let's hope this matter gets resolved, and they can move on to other things." She hesitated a moment, thinking. "Is that why Logan's not here?"

"He got called out on another job. Levi often has half-a-dozen to a dozen jobs happening all at once."

"The logistics of that must be a nightmare."

"Maybe, but I'm sure he's used to it by now. And, with Ice there, and any number of other very capable people, I'm sure they all handle it just fine." Jace picked up the wine bottle and refilled her glass; then he filled his.

"Are you enjoying staying with them?"

Jace shrugged. "I haven't been there long enough to know. But, while I have been there, it's been good. I like the people. I like the sense of camaraderie. I like doing jobs that help others. What's not to like?"

She nodded. "Just think. I would never have met you if you weren't working for Levi and Ice."

He lifted his wineglass and gave her a crooked smile. "I'll drink to that."

Once again they were right back to that same charged atmosphere, as if only the two of them were in the entire world.

IT WAS ALL Jace could do to pull his gaze from the beautiful woman across from him. Attraction sparkled in the air, giving a heavy, husky feeling to the moment. He lifted his wine and drained it. He motioned to her glass and whispered, "Are you going to finish that?"

She smiled. "I will."

He hadn't expected this level of attraction.

She took a big shaky breath and said, "Do you think something is wrong with me because I had a relationship with those three men?"

He shook his head. "No. Why would I?"

She gave him a tremulous smile. "Glad to hear that, but it is so weird to have it all laid out on paper. Looks as if I went from one man to the other two."

He studied her for a long moment. "Are you ashamed of the relationships?"

She shook her head. "No." She shrugged. "Even though the relationships didn't last, they were all such great people. Just not quite right for me."

"It never occurred to me," he said honestly. "I haven't been lacking in relationships for the last twelve years myself."

She chuckled. "A beautiful man like you, I have no doubt you're never lacking for partners."

He sat back and gave her a crooked grin. "I'm currently single. Let's make that clear."

"Oh my." She tilted her head. "When was your last relationship?"

"Ended about six months ago."

"Any particular reason?"

"She went back to her ex-boyfriend."

Emily's eyebrows shot up. "Well, that's an interesting reason."

"I came into her life when she wasn't ready for somebody new."

"Were you terribly upset?"

"No." A sly smile slipped out. "And that's how I knew she was probably better off."

Emily chuckled. "Not all relationships end quite so nicely."

"Your last one?"

"Somebody at work. We parted amicably. He took a job in a different city."

"Did you break up with him over the move?"

"He asked for the transfer. We broke up as part of his move to a new life. I wasn't bothered either." She picked up her glass and swirled the red wine. "In a way it was nice to have somebody to do something with."

"A lot of relationships are like that. People fall into them because they want to do something. They don't want to be alone all the time."

She nodded. "I still can't quite imagine somebody leaving you for an old boyfriend."

He laughed. "It happens. As a SEAL, I wasn't around all that much. Since leaving the military, I was hoping, more often than not, that I'd be around more. I stayed at a friend's family home after his brother was in an accident. He had gone home to help his father and brother run the ranch until his brother was back on his feet. I went to help them out. My whole unit is looking for a reason to carry on. Finding a purpose took a little bit more time."

"A ranch should have been fun," Emily said. "Particularly if it was new to you."

"I had been to Rory's place a couple times. He had stayed for months on end and helped out, day in and day out. It was a relentless experience." He outstretched his hand across the table toward her and opened his palm.

She took it without hesitation.

"I kind of thought maybe I would meet somebody there. I met several women in town, but I didn't feel anything. I was going through that stage of life where nothing mattered anymore. Yet being at Rory's place gave me purpose. Then I met a bunch of women after Katie and I broke up. I went out with a couple of them, just a few dates each, but I can't say I felt the attraction I was hoping for."

"What were you hoping for?" Emily sensed her voice deepening to a husky whisper.

He raised his gaze slowly and studied her face. "Something like what I feel for you." He watched the surprise come into her beautiful blue eyes. He leaned forward. "And I know you feel it too."

He didn't know how it happened or who made the first move. Before he truly understood anything, she was in his arms, and he was kissing her like there was no tomorrow. Maybe that was because, in his world, there often wasn't.

Chapter 10

EMILY TIGHTENED HER arms around his neck and kissed Jace back with all the longing inside her heart. She hadn't expected this to happen. Maybe on the inside she'd hoped it would, but hope was a long way away from reality. She knew she could certainly work the angles to get them in bed. However, starting an affair was not the same thing as knowing they already had a connection between the two of them and at such a level. And that was what she wanted. His character had so much depth to it that she knew she wouldn't get tired of finding out more about him. He was gentle, caring. A lot could be said for that can-do attitude of his, all packaged up in a quiet deep exterior. He was very protective. Very caring. Very special.

When she slowly pulled her head away, she stroked his cheekbones and his nose. When her thumbs dropped to gently follow the curve of his lips, they quirked into her ministrations, and he kissed her thumb pads, almost nipping at her skin.

She chuckled. "Do you bite?"

He hugged her close and whispered, "I might nibble a little bit, but I'd never hurt you."

She tilted her head and searched his gaze. Feeling daring and realizing she hadn't known him long but unable to resist the lure of attraction, the promise of passion, she slid her arms around his neck again, her fingers sliding along his scalp, and whispered, "Stay with me tonight."

He kissed her temple, trailing warm delicate kisses across her eyes, the tip of her nose, and then a whispering feather of a kiss across her lips. "Are you sure?"

"I can't say I have ever had a man question my invitation."

The rumble of laughter that rolled up through his chest made her smile. He was so damn big. He was like a big quiet teddy bear. When his arms wrapped around her, holding her close, she knew how perfect he was. She couldn't wait to make love with him. To have that intense focus turned on her … Was she deceiving herself? Was it what she thought was between them? Or was she reading this all wrong?

"It is fast," she murmured, hating that common sense was forcing its way through her mind. Her body didn't want to be sensible. Her heart didn't want to have second thoughts. Her mind and soul needed to feel, to move past all this death, move past all this nastiness, to something joyous. She slid her hands down his arms and then back up again. She smiled and said in a low tone, "Help me forget the ugliness."

He tilted her chin up and lowered his head. His kiss was teasing—light. Her response was anything but. When he swung her into his arms and carried her to the bedroom, it was just perfect. He set her down on top of the bed, his hands already sliding under her shirt, coming to her bra strap seconds later. Both items disappeared under his expert touch. Then they were kneeling on the bed, holding each other close. Hot skin to hot skin.

She laughed. "Well now, that was fast."

He gave her a slow smile and whispered, "Hell no, it

wasn't. You still have on clothes."

She tilted her head and challenged, "So do you."

He'd left his shoes at the front door when she'd let him in. As she watched in fascination, he stepped off the bed, his jeans fell to the floor, and, a moment later, he stood before her completely nude. Completely at home in his physical body. Lord, she loved that about him. So full of self-confidence. His movements had a complete naturalness to them—all of them. And then of course there was his erection waving at her.

She reached out a hand, but he took a step back.

"Now who's wearing too many clothes?"

She shuddered with need. Glancing down, she let out a breath and, in a flurry, freed herself of every last stitch. Even her thong went flying. Now she stood before him as nude as he was.

With a glance at the bed, she tugged the covers down to the foot. She went to sit down, only to find him already stretched out before her, his arms open and waiting.

She kneeled across the bed and came to him. She didn't know where her normal shyness was. Her mother would be shocked at her lack of modesty. Then again, she hadn't found holding back to be a blessing in any way. And, if Jace would show up in this relationship with as much honesty as he'd shown so far, she could do no less. He gave a tug, pulling her atop his heavily muscled body. She shuddered as her skin, already sensitized, overloaded as all her nerve endings came to life. He was so damn hot. She stroked a hand over his chest, loving the defined muscles over his ribs, and, as she drew her fingers across his belly, his six-pack showed up as he clenched his muscles.

She chuckled. "You are so beautiful," she declared.

When he remained silent, she glanced up to find him studying her with a look of surprise in his eyes. She grinned. "I mean that. You're seriously beautiful."

He shook his head, pulled her toward him, and whispered, "You're the beautiful one. Inside and out."

His lips met hers in a gentle touch that quickly became possessive, demanding a response. She stretched across him, her hands busy in his hair, sliding through his curls, teasing, stroking, caressing. She lifted her head and kissed him again and again and again. She couldn't get enough.

He rolled over, pinning her in place. This time when he kissed her, it was long, deep, drugging, an open-mouth kiss that left her weak and limp in his arms.

When he raised his lips to drift across her cheeks and down her neck, it was all she could do to whisper, "Wow."

Instead of answering, he shuddered and kissed her again, his tongue sliding inside, finding an immediate response. She sank to depths of passion she'd never experienced before. Her body twisted and arched against him in a way she didn't recognize. Nothing was hidden between them, and yet so much was unknown.

He appeared determined to explore every inch of her. She'd never felt so loved, so cosseted, as he teased and stroked, caressed and admired the valleys and curves of her body. When his lips followed the same trail his fingers had gone, she sighed and moaned, then laughed at the tickle spots and cried when he left her wanting more. He slid between her open thighs. She gasped, her hips automatically rising. As he drank deep from the heart of her, her whimpers of joy filled the room. But he wouldn't let her climax like that. She lay panting on the bed, sprawled open before him, moaning for more.

When he rose up above her, he slid his hands under her butt cheeks and lifted her, pulling her higher against him. And then he slid inside and all the way home. She gasped at the invasion, the depth and the width of him stretching her, pinning her in place, holding her, … possessing her.

He tilted his head back, struggling for control, his hands gripping her hips to hold her still. She watched the ripples moving along his body, seeing the passion in his flushed cheeks and tense jawline. It was such a pleasure to watch him, reveling in his own passion, at his own delight in being here with her.

Then he let out a long slow breath, opened his eyes, and grinned at her. He cupped her breasts, his fingers gentle as they tugged on the nipples. He cupped, weighed, and measured them before leaning over and taking one of the nipples deep into his mouth and suckling hard. Her hips arched yet again, but there was no place for them to go as he leaned over her, bent at the waist, keeping her pinned as he tasted the bounty before him.

She tugged his head up and kissed him, a deep drugging kiss, and still he wouldn't move. Frustrated she tried to raise her hips to get him to shift, but he wasn't having any of it. Finally she grasped his head, tilted his face, and glared at him. "Move, dammit, move."

He gave a bark of laughter and thrust his hips forward. She arched her back as he slammed home again and again and again. A kaleidoscope of colors and sensations exploded within. But it didn't stop there. As one ripple ended, another began. She went from one climax right into another. Helpless, she lay in his arms as he pounded deep inside her, taking and giving pleasure for pleasure. She was helpless in the storm of his passion, her own rising and falling with every movement he made.

Finally he shifted her position ever-so-slightly, wrapped her thighs around his hips, and plunged in one more time— hard and so very deep. And he shuddered above her, his arms shaking, his face contorting as his own climax ripped through him. She couldn't help but watch, loving that she brought him to this. Loving that he was here in her arms at this moment.

JACE SLID TO the side and tucked her up against him.

"So good," he murmured against her temple as he slowly stroked up and down her back. Was there ever a feeling quite like this? His body throbbed with a satisfaction that went bone deep. He didn't want this moment to end. She just had to give him a few minutes more to lie here and enjoy. Then he'd happily start all over again. No way was his body done for the night. It'd been too long, and she was too damn perfect.

"Talk about transporting me to a fantasy world away from the reality I'm currently living," she said on a happy sigh.

A chuckle rumbled from his chest. "Maybe we can keep you in a fantasy world for most of the night."

At that she propped herself up on her elbows on his chest and grinned at him. "Do I not need sleep tonight?"

"Well, tomorrow is Friday. So, by right, you have a weekend off to recuperate in case you are a little low on energy tomorrow," he said. He tugged her closer into his arms and hugged her tight.

"I'm so glad Logan left you behind."

"Me too." He kissed her forehead and then her cheek,

his body already waking up within seconds. He slipped her onto her back gently and slid inside.

She gasped and arched in his arms, her eyes closing. "So damn good," she murmured.

He cupped her breasts, loving her soft skin. He bent down and gave them his undivided attention. All the while he kept her hips tight against his, their bodies sealed together as one. Slowly, gently, each stroke more of a caress, he pushed her closer to the edge again. The second joining didn't have the same volatile excitement as the first. This was more about a meeting of minds and hearts, their bodies, the hunger, already at peace. This time it was more for them. He didn't want to waste a moment of this special connection.

With a cry, she arched in his arms, calling his name. She collapsed onto the bed as he joined her over the cliff. With the afterglow still running through his bones, he wondered if anything was sweeter.

He gathered her in his arms, and she whispered, "I might need to sleep for a bit."

He brushed his lips gently against hers and whispered, "Sleep. I'll be here when you wake up."

She snuggled in, her body fitting itself naturally to the curves of his. "Promise?"

He smiled. "I promise."

Chapter 11

EMILY WOKE IN the night, her body turning to find Jace there, waiting for her. She didn't know how many times they'd made love, but it seemed endless. Never had she made love like that. Never had she felt more welcomed. Never had she been more in tune with a man as she did with him. By the time the sun rose on the horizon, her body was exhausted, her mind fatigued. But her heart was so full that there were almost tears in her eyes from the overflow.

"It's only five."

"I don't know if it's worth sleeping for an hour or if I should get up and take a shower," she said, her voice a little raspy.

He pulled her closer and whispered, "Sleep." His hands were already stroking her breasts, sliding across her belly to her hips as if afraid that he didn't touch her, he would lose contact with her. Almost memorizing every curve ...

"I'm scared too. It's like the daylight will change everything. You'll be gone. This horrible case will still be on my desk." She shook her head. "No, I'm scared to go to sleep."

"Then we won't," he whispered and rose above her once again.

She marveled at his endurance. She wondered that she could still want him after so many times in the night. She loved how he was always there, ready, wanting her in return.

But, for all her wishes to stay awake, when her body finally collapsed yet again, she was asleep before her head hit the pillow. Instead of warm lovely dreams from her night of passion, nightmares followed her. Men drowning. Men dying all around her. The men in her past, the men in her future.

She woke with a heavy heart. A restless urge was inside, an abrasive sandpaper against her awareness. She sat upright and looked around. Jace slept quietly beside her. Or at least he lay beside her. She wasn't at all sure he slept. As she stared at him, she studied the long length of his lashes against his cheek, so ridiculously long that every woman would be jealous. She reached down, her fingers gently stroking his whiskered chin and hollowed cheeks, even as he slept. He was a lean, mean fighting machine. She could imagine he'd done a fair bit of damage in his military days. He was no slouch now. Everywhere she looked, he had angles and muscles, just an amazing male in his prime. He was spectacular.

"Are you watching me sleep?" he asked without opening his eyes.

She leaned over and kissed his lips. "I'm enjoying how absolutely stunning you are."

His lips quirked, the little dimple appeared, making her heart twitch in response. She'd never forget this evening.

"I don't want this night to end," she whispered.

"Do you want a repeat tonight? Same time? Same place?" he asked, slowly opening his eyes, giving him that sexy I-can-do-this-all-day-and-all-night look. Her body softened, knowing what it wanted the most was right here for the asking. So damn ready to welcome him back into her body again.

She shuddered. "You're lethal. With just a glance, my body already wants to crawl down there with you."

"Do you have to go? Can you call and tell them you'll be late this morning?"

She gave him a stern look. "It's already late. And aren't you're supposed to be doing something too?"

"What time is it?"

"It's after eight."

His eyes widened in surprise. He contemplated her for a moment and then said, "We might have time for a shower together."

She chuckled. "I know you think you're good, but ..." And his smile made her heart hitch.

He whispered, "I used be a SEAL. We're known for our water skills." He stood, grabbed her, tossed her over his shoulder, and walked into the bathroom—while she screamed in delight. The side of his thick muscled shoulder scrunched beneath her as her hands slid down, reaching as far she could, gently stroking his back with her nails. He set her smoothly on her feet, immediately followed by warm water sliding down her body. She gasped, then sighed happily as he reached for the shampoo and gently worked the lather through her hair, softly massaging her scalp, cleaning her long locks, stroking her head.

"Oh, my God, that feels so good."

In a throaty voice he said, "For some reason, I feel like I've heard that a few times through the night."

A laugh bubbled out of her. "You sure did. So show me all over again."

And he did.

By the time they made it out of the shower, wrapped in towels, and she put coffee on, she knew it didn't matter what kind of shit happened for the rest of her day. She was already having the best day she possibly could. She was exhausted, but it didn't matter one bit.

He drove off, leaving her standing there waving goodbye with a silly look on her face. She got into her own vehicle and drove to the office. As she approached the front door, she found Wilson there, holding the door open. A fatherly look was on his face as he studied her features. "Is there something you want to tell me?"

She shook her head. "Absolutely not. You might have five kids, but no way will I discuss last night."

Wilson looked at his watch.

She grinned and darted ahead of him. Hopefully coffee was on. If not, she would have to make some for herself. She'd need it to get through the day.

She turned on her computer, walked to the coffeepot, grabbed a cup, filled it, headed back to her desk to find her in-box full and getting fuller as everything downloaded. Frowning, she collapsed into her chair and started her day.

At the top of her in-box was an email from Ice. She opened that first. She recognized two names. She pulled up her database, checked out both names and realized they both had a life insurance policy with her company. She picked up the phone, called Ice, and said, "Why do those two names matter?"

"I'm hoping they don't. Jace will talk to them this morning. We need to make sure both men are safe," Ice said.

Terrified by what she meant, Emily checked the details on the policies. One million dollars, like the others. Her hand shaking, she wrote down the names and details and returned to the database. She had sorted all the policies in the Austin and surrounding areas that involved a TxSAR volunteer and that had a one-million-dollar policy. Three had come back. Two of them were the names Ice had given her. The third one wasn't on the list.

Her own personal honor code said she had to do something, but what the hell was she supposed to do? She grabbed her notepad, stood, and walked into Wilson's office. She closed the door and sat down in front of his desk. "Wilson, we have to talk."

JACE HAD PARKED outside the TxSAR Center when his phone went off. "Good morning, Ice. What's up?"

"I gave Emily two names to run a few minutes ago. Both of them have policies. You need to talk to them."

"I'm at the center right now. If you find anybody else, give me a shout." He got out of the truck and slammed the door shut.

"Call me as soon as you're done," Ice said tersely.

"Will do." Jace pocketed his phone and stepped through the front entrance of the center. A group of men were off to one side, learning ropes and knots. Somebody else stood off to the left, stacking lifejackets, checking them over. Yet another group looked at the harnesses. Jace was glad to see it. They could do only as much as was humanly possible to save somebody, but old broken equipment made it almost impossible. Jace walked toward the front counter and smiled at Amber. She took one look at him, and her smile fell away.

He hated that, but there was no help for it. "I wanted to speak with Bill and Frank, if they're in this morning," he said gently.

Relieved, she nodded. "Yeah, they are. Hang on. I'll get them."

She disappeared into the back. When she returned a few minutes later, two big strapping young men come out behind her. They shook hands with Jace. He looked around and asked, "Is there a private place where we can talk?"

Bill nodded. "Come on in the back."

They took him to the room he'd been in last time. With the door shut, they sat down, and he asked them many of the questions he'd asked the rest of the team. Bill hadn't been at the scene. He'd arrived later when they'd already lost track of Ronnie and Howard. Frank had been there. He'd been helping the woman and the little kids out of the van. He hadn't seen Ronnie. The first he realized there was a problem was when screams came from the shoreline, and he realized they'd seen Ronnie pop up farther down the raging river.

"We have no idea what happened. As far as we knew, everything was as it always had been."

"By the way, do you guys have life insurance policies? I mean, it's dangerous work."

Bill nodded. "I have a policy in case anything happens to me," he said. "My wife would have a tough time being left alone with three kids."

"The same for me too."

"Did you buy them all around the same time?"

Bill shook his head. "I don't think so. I know I had a talk with Troy about it when I first signed on. At the time I was pretty cocky. But we've lost three men in the last year and a half," he said. "So my policy is relatively new. I want to save my wife any financial hardship."

"I don't have a wife and kids," Frank said. "But my sister's a single mom with four kids. One of my bimonthly paychecks goes to help keep a roof over her head. I'm in IT and can afford to help her. And she needs my support right now. Anything happens to me, well …" He glanced toward the door and said, "I guess a lot of people have life insurance here, don't they?"

"Some do. Some don't. Not a lot of people believe in it. Both Ronnie and Howard did though."

"Good, considering what happened."

Jace stood and shook the men's hands. "Sorry to disturb you guys. I need to speak with one more volunteer, and then I should be done." He glanced at his notes and said, "I'm looking for John."

"Yeah, we haven't seen that much of him since Ronnie died. They were tight."

Jace frowned. "Maybe I'll call him. He might meet me for coffee somewhere instead. Coming here might make it harder on him."

Back at the truck, he phoned Ice and gave her an update. "I'll call this John guy, maybe run by his place."

She sent the phone number. He clicked on it and waited until it rang. A man answered. Jace explained who he was and that he was interviewing everybody at the center about Ronnie's and Howard's deaths.

"Sorry. I haven't been around much lately. But I can't stand Troy. And Ronnie, well, he was the best damn leader we had."

"What about the leader you lost last year?"

"Ken was pretty good. But there was something wonderful about Ronnie. And, even if he wasn't there, we should have had Howard, and that would have been fine too. Ronnie and Howard were both cut from the same cloth. Both were good to have your back."

"And Troy?"

"He's filling in for me. I'm supposed to be in charge

now. But, … well, I'm not sure I can do the job. Still, he's not the same leader as the others. It's kind of hard to see three damn good men go down and leave someone like Troy in charge."

"Why can't you take over?"

"I don't have the heart for it anymore," John said quietly. "I'm not sure I'll do this kind of volunteer work again. It's almost like I've done my time. Losing three of my good friends, well, a little voice in the back of my head keeps saying, *You could be next.*"

Jace understood that. It was the first sign of a man losing his heart. "Then maybe it is time," he said softly. "You've got a wife and children. Stick close to them. Because they could be the reason you stay alive."

"Do you still need to meet with me?"

"If you're willing to answer a few questions on the phone right now, that will be okay."

"Sure. Otherwise, if you want, you can come here. My wife has gone to work. I should be at the TxSAR Center, but, well, like I said, things have been difficult for me."

"Can you give me your address?" Jace wrote it down and listened to his directions. The drive was five minutes from where he was.

A few minutes later he pulled up to an apartment building. John lived on the ground floor. Jace knocked at the door and smiled as an older man answered it.

After they shook hands, John invited him in. They sat at the kitchen table and had coffee. "Do you know how long Ronnie was in the water?"

"No. We were all busy, getting as many people out as we could, and, although we keep an eye on our team, we rarely time the rescues. The water was rising steadily …" He shook his head. "Sometimes I don't sleep at night, remembering it." He glanced at Jace. "You've got military experience, don't you?"

Jace nodded. "I know exactly what you mean about the nightmares. Some things you never forget."

"I think I should go to a therapist for help," he said with a broken laugh. "It's not just that. It's the whole damn thing. It's so wrong that Ronnie and Howard both died like that."

"It can happen to anyone." Jace watched the older man's face carefully. Sad acceptance confirmed what he thought.

"Oh, yes. Ropes can get caught. Hooks can snap free. Sometimes we make decisions to hook up people we're rescuing, and our own ropes are not attached. We're not supposed to do it, but I've done it. I know Ronnie's done it."

"You know anybody with photos from the accident site, or any when Ronnie's body was brought in?"

"I imagine the police do. Have you talked to them?"

Jace nodded. "His gear was already partially off when he was brought in. The safety harnesses had been removed when they brought him to the morgue."

"Yeah, those suckers are expensive. Besides, Ronnie didn't need his anymore."

"Did you see if his rope got caught?"

John shook his head. "I didn't, no."

For a second Jace turned his gaze away from John's face. "Did you go to his funeral?"

"Yes. But I didn't say anything to his wife." He glanced at Jace. "It makes me look like a coward, but I wasn't ready to say goodbye." John's eyes filled with tears. He shook his head. "Look at me. I'm just a weepy old man here."

"There's a whole lot worse things than to mourn for your friend. Imagine if nobody mourned for Ronnie. What kind of a world would that be? He and Howard were always there, helping out. They loved volunteering. They died helping others. That deserves our respect."

"True. Ronnie and Howard both were well-loved."

Jace stood and walked to the door. "Thanks for speaking with me." He hesitated a moment. "By the way, do you have a life insurance policy? It's a question I'm asking everybody. It's a dangerous business you are in. I wondered how many of you look to protect the families you leave behind."

"I didn't. But after Ronnie's death, I signed up for one." He shrugged. "I feel stupid doing so now because I'm not sure about going back. I feel like I've lost my edge."

"Maybe you haven't lost it. Maybe you can't find it for the moment. Grieve first, say goodbye to your friends, and then remember all the people they rescued, all the people you saved over these years. You might decide you need to be a part of that again. It's your decision. The thing is, you can't do what is right for everybody else. You must do what's right for you."

John smiled. "I'm glad you came by this morning. I feel much better."

"Good."

The two men shook hands, and Jace headed to his truck. As soon as he was in the driver's seat, his phone rang. It was Ice. "John was at home. He's still having trouble dealing with the loss of his friends," Jace said, then relayed the little bit of information he got from John. "He did just take out a life insurance policy. But it's with Prescott Health."

"You didn't ask him how much it was for, did you?"

"No, I never thought to." He glanced back at the house. "Do you want me to go back and ask him?"

"No, it's probably not an issue." Her voice sounded distracted. "Look. I'll call you back. Things are kind of busy here at the moment."

He hung up the phone and sat in the truck for a long moment, thinking about everything. So far nothing had made him change his mind about his earlier theory. But how could he prove it? How did he prove somebody was killing off these men for an insurance payday?

He shook his head, started up the truck, and drove to his hotel room. He wasn't sure if it was still booked for today or not. Ice had told him to come home today, and check out was at eleven o'clock. It was almost that time now. As he walked inside, he got a text from Ice.

Stay in town for the day. Keep the hotel for another night, and we'll see where we're at in the morning.

He stood at the front desk and thought about that for a long moment. He walked off to the side, pulled out his phone again, and called Emily. When he heard her voice, he smiled. "So is that offer good for tonight, or do I book my hotel room again?"

She chuckled. "Well, if you're booking a hotel for another night, then I'm coming there. But it seems silly to spend all that money when my place has a warm bed."

"Done," he said with a grin. "You available for lunch today?"

"Absolutely. I wanted to invite you out. I was afraid you would leave, and we wouldn't get a chance to say goodbye."

"I'm staying in town for the day, unless my orders change," he said. "But I'd like to spend lunch with you anyway. Tomorrow will come soon enough."

"So you pick where we go this time," she said. "Meet

you in front in an hour."

He grinned and spoke to the receptionist. "I'm here to check out."

The woman nodded and started the paperwork. Inside he was delighted. As far as he was concerned, today was a great day. Who'd have thought he'd get a second night with Emily before he had to return to the compound?

Chapter 12

EMILY'S CONVERSATION WITH Wilson had been intense, with him toeing the company line. Only when she threatened to contact the cops about it did he agree to talk to the head office again.

He warned her, "You know your job is on the line over this."

She nodded. "That may be, but so are my ethics and honor. I don't know for sure that anyone else is in danger, but, if we don't tell the cops what's going on, and something does happen, we are ultimately responsible."

"That's not fair," he protested. "Like you said, you found no evidence anything is going on."

She gave him a steely smile. "Make the call." She got up and returned to her desk. She closed her eyes to regain some sense of equilibrium. It was damn hard. She wasn't sure what she was supposed to do now. Wilson was right in that they knew essentially nothing.

It was almost time to go for lunch, and, for that, she was grateful. She shouldn't tell Jace anything, but it would be hard not to.

Sitting at her desk was useless when she could be standing outside, trying to calm down for that extra five minutes. She gathered up her purse and her sweater, logged off her computer, and locked up her desk. Outside she paced, her fingers shoved deep into her sweater pockets as she mulled things over.

There was an all-too-real possibility that she would end up looking for a new job. And that was both sad and exhilarating. Maybe the company would offer her a position in a different department. But did she want to stay even then?

Every time a vehicle pulled up, she turned to see if it was Jace. Each time the vehicle either drove off or turned into the parking lot, she groaned out loud. "Come on, Jace. I need to get away from here."

At those words, he pulled up. She smiled, and, before he had a chance to turn off the engine, she opened the door and hopped in. "Let's go," she said.

He shot her a startled look. "Are you in a hurry?" He turned to check the traffic and then pulled the truck onto the main road.

"No, and yes. Another argument with my boss about a discussion with the head office. I might not have a job when I get back." She shrugged. "I need to get away right now."

Heavy silence filled the cab for a moment. "Something we did?"

"Not directly. It's this whole case. I want to do something, and they won't let me."

Jace nodded. "Did you tell the cops what we found?"

It was her turn to shoot him a surprised glance. "You understand I can't talk about it, right?" Her voice was tight.

"I know. Given that you're a little on the stressed side, you should have a glass of wine with lunch."

"Sounds good." In her mind she was thinking a couple stiff drinks might be a better idea. But she didn't dare go back to work with alcohol on her breath. "And considering we didn't have breakfast, I'm more than ready for some real food."

He pulled into a popular chain restaurant parking lot. "Will this do?"

"Absolutely. I could get into a big burger right now."

He smiled. "A woman after my own heart."

He wrapped an arm around her shoulders and gently tugged her close. She turned and wrapped her arms around him and burrowed deep. He held her, not saying anything, gently stroking her back and waiting.

Finally she could breathe normally. She pulled away and looked at him. "Thank you. For being you."

"I'm glad I'm here," he said seriously. "As you well know, my time can be cut short at any moment."

"I know. I guess that's why I'm even more appreciative of the fact that you're here with me now."

He led her inside and asked for a booth in the far corner. There he let her sit with her back to the rest of the restaurant while he sat facing her. She studied his position and smiled. "So is our seating so you can see if anybody's coming? Or is it so you can see if we're safe?"

He slanted a look at her. "Does it make a difference?" His tone was light and playful but underneath was a serious tone.

She narrowed her gaze. "Did you stir up a hornet's nest?"

His smile was bland, the look in his eyes even more so. "I don't know what you're talking about."

Then the waitress arrived. She handed out menus and asked if they'd like anything to drink. He ordered a carafe of wine for Emily. Then he quickly corrected his order. "Make that one glass, please."

The waitress nodded and hurried away. Knowing Jace wouldn't explain his actions any more than she could explain her morning, she chose to delve into the menu. There she found the chef's burger. She read all the ingredients as she felt her appetite rising to the forefront. That was a good sign. When she was stressed, she had no appetite, even tended to forget about food. The sandwich sounded so good. She closed her menu and said, "I know what I'm having."

He glanced at her and said, "A chef's burger with a Caesar salad on the side."

"How did you know?"

He smiled. "I want the same, only with fries." The waitress returned with a glass of wine. He ordered two chef's burgers, making the substitution for salad on hers. When they were finally alone again, he nodded to the wine. "Take a sip. It will help you relax."

She laughed. "The hug did the most good yet."

He gave her a slow dawning smile that sent her pulse racing. "If you could take the afternoon off," he said suggestively, "I can do a whole lot more than a hug."

She let her breath out slowly. "Oh, you are deadly." She shook her head. "I might end up being forced to have the afternoon off. But I'll go back in case I still have a job."

"That bad?"

"Yes," she said. "That bad."

"Is it wrong of me to think maybe that's a good thing?"

She set down her wine and stared at him. "That I get fired is a good thing?"

He shook his head. "Obviously not that part. But a new beginning. How do you feel about a new city?"

She snorted. "You mean, a city like Houston by any chance?" She watched in amazement as color washed up his neck. He dropped his gaze and stared at the table, his fingers folding the napkin in some complicated pattern. She leaned forward. "Are you too embarrassed to talk about it?"

As he raised his head, she saw his discomfort. "This is where your home is. And I don't have any right to ask you to move."

"It's hardly a move. Sure it's another city and another apartment I'd have to find and all the headaches that go with that. But I might already need to find a new job." She shrugged. "It's not that far out of the realm of possibilities."

"I don't want you to move because of me."

"Can you move your job?"

He frowned. "I could move anywhere in the Houston area. Any farther than that would be hard, if not impossible."

She nodded. "Well, I'll consider it. It could be, when I return to the office, that things are fine." But she doubted it. She'd basically issued a threat against the company. And there were names for people who did that. *Whistleblower* came to mind. She didn't know for a fact that this had anything to do with the records being hacked. But she would be pretty upset if somebody else was hurt because she hadn't stepped up and said something.

The rest of the lunch hour passed while discussing more neutral topics, and, when it was finally time to leave, she let him pick up the tab.

When he dropped her off at the front door, he asked, "You want me to wait?"

She gave him a brave smile. "No, my vehicle is here."

She walked to the front door, which was locked, used her security pass, but nothing happened. She swiped her card a second time, and again nothing happened. She bowed her head.

"I guess that's my answer."

HE HATED TO drop her off at the office. He didn't have a purpose in his own current direction. But it felt wrong for him and Emily to leave off there. He hadn't gotten more than five blocks away when his instincts wouldn't let him keep going. Checking his rearview mirror, he pulled a fast U-turn in the middle of the road and drove back. He parked on the far side from the office building only to find Emily standing dejectedly outside the building's front door.

Oh, shit.

He hopped out, raced across the road, and called out, "Can't you get in?"

He loved the way her face lit up with joy at seeing him. That was what he had been missing for so long. Knowing somebody out there cared for him like he did for her. He knew they only had a fledgling romance, and so many things could go wrong. But he really liked who she was inside and out. The passion between them was a great start. And he knew that, if nurtured, it could take them the distance and be something so much stronger. He had to foster that strength. She reached out a hand for him, and he took it.

"The door's locked," she said.

"Come on," he urged. "No point standing here, wondering if you're fired or locked out. Find out for sure."

She nodded, took out her phone, and dialed. "I feel like he would do this though. No confrontation is involved this way."

"What about your personal stuff?"

She shook her head. "I brought my purse and sweater with me. I left an apple and maybe a granola bar in my drawer. That's all."

"Did you need any information? Should you leave any last notes or anything on your files?"

"I finished updating my files this morning. Two huge stacks remain to be done, another set on my desk. That will no longer be my problem." She shrugged. "He's not answering."

He pulled out his phone, took the number off her phone, and asked, "What's the chance he's not answering because it's you calling?"

She snorted. "That would be like him."

He hit the Dial button and held it up between them. "If he answers, you take my phone and talk to him," he said.

Sure enough Wilson's voice came on a moment later. "Hello, who is this?"

She snatched the phone from Jace's hand and walked a few steps away. "Wilson, this is Emily."

Jace walked the other direction to give her a little privacy. This was a complication he hadn't expected. When they talked about her possibly losing her job over lunch, it hadn't seemed as real or as close as it appeared to be. He could hope, for her sake, that she still had her job, but he well knew what it took to walk away when your morals and ethics came into play. That's why he and so many of his friends had all walked away from the military. If she did the same thing, well, he certainly couldn't blame her for it. In fact he admired her all that much more. But that left him with a bit of a hole in his world. She would need help and likely quickly.

He waited another few minutes, keeping an eye on Emily's face as she paced. He blocked out what conversation he could hear, but it was hard to miss bits and pieces. Finally she turned toward him and handed him his phone.

"I've been let go," she said with a sneer. "They didn't want to fire me in case I decide to contest that."

He nodded. "They want their company name clear of this mess."

She nodded. "And I understand that. But people are dying."

"And, in all fairness, it may not have anything to do with the life insurance policies. Or directly related to the previous hack of the insurance records."

She nodded. "And yet they didn't do anything about the breach in the security. Some people have no idea their information was accessed." She shrugged. "And I don't know if that's a criminal matter or not. But I lost my job over it." For a moment she looked completely lost. Then she gave herself a head shake and smiled. "Well, here's to a whole new beginning."

The look on her face said she wasn't exactly looking forward to that. This might be a new beginning, but she hadn't planned on it. And, when it wasn't her own choice, her adjustment could take a bit.

She gave him a bright smile. "I didn't know going in that this was a potential end result, but I had a feeling as the investigation went on that it could be."

He nodded and stayed quiet.

Her bottom lip trembled. "I hadn't expected it to happen so fast."

He nodded again. When her lip continued to tremble, he opened his arms. She rushed into them, and he held her close. If there was one thing he could do for her, it was stand by her side, at least for however long he was here.

Chapter 13

SHE LET GO so he could answer his phone and wiped her eyes, grateful she wasn't completely breaking down in tears. She had known this was a possible outcome. But had held out hope that morality and humanity were more important than the corporate mentality. But of course the corporate mind-set had won out. They wanted to make sure she couldn't access anything else. Well, that was fine.

Sometimes you must take a stand, and she'd made hers. She turned to study the building. She couldn't see anybody, which meant she had no chance to say goodbye to any of those she'd worked with. Although she had their contact information. She also had contacts in other companies. She could possibly get a job with any of them. But, if they looked for references, well, then she was screwed. It was a scary position to be in, but she hadn't spent much money for the last few years, so her bank account was looking healthy. She didn't own her apartment, so she would move as soon as she gave notice. It was such a big world out there. She'd been relatively happy in her small corner. She didn't have a clue what she would do next, where she would go.

"Ready to leave?"

She glanced at Jace. "Where to?"

"I suggest we drive your vehicle home, park it at your place. Then you can spend the rest of the afternoon with me.

At this point, I have tracked down everybody from the center who was at the river, even some who weren't. I want to return to the accident site one more time and also stop by the police station."

She smiled. "Sounds like the perfect way to spend my first afternoon free. With you. I haven't had a free afternoon in a long time."

"Will you get a severance package?"

"The same one I signed for when I joined. I get one month's wages." She shrugged. "I'll be fine."

"I'm sorry you have to suffer for it." He walked her to the parking lot. "Let's get your vehicle out of here. Technically it's not allowed to be here since this is private property."

She raised her eyebrows. "I never thought about that. You'll follow me to my place then?"

He nodded. "Yes."

She hopped into her car, reversed out of her spot, and, with one last look at the building she had worked in for the last four years, drove onto the main road. Jace pulled in behind her. She loved that about him.

Her place wasn't very far away, and the traffic was minimal. It was early afternoon. She kind of wanted to go inside alone but knew she'd probably get depressed or angry, and neither was a good solution. It was much better that she spend the time with Jace that they had. And honestly she would do that anyway as she assumed it might be her last opportunity. Now that she was a free agent, she had some decisions to make too.

She got out of her vehicle, walked into her apartment building. He was there already waiting for her.

"Do you need to go upstairs? Do you want to get changed?"

She sent him a saucy grin. "Are you trying to get me out of my clothes already?"

That startled a grin out of him. "Nothing I'd like better," he said, "but I do have work to do this afternoon."

She nodded and walked toward him, her purse in hand. "Then let's go. I will be your assistant for the day."

He chuckled, holding out a hand. She slipped hers in it, and together they walked to his truck parked at the curb. Then he headed toward the police department. Once at the station, with her as quiet as possible, they sat down as the detective retrieved his file.

"I don't understand exactly what we're looking for," Detective Dickerson said, holding on to the file.

"To see the ends of the ropes securing the two dead men. I understood Ronnie's lifeline had been cut, but I wanted to see how jagged they were myself. I know it's been fixed now but wondered if you have any images of the ends when they came out of the river? Of his cousin's rope?"

The detective sat. "We're back to that issue Ice was talking about, right?"

Jace nodded. "I want to ensure these men died by accident, not by somebody else's hand."

"I don't think I have a picture of the ropes." He opened his file and went through it. Then he brought up the case file on the computer. "These are the crime scene photos but only of the body. Don't forget the weather was completely shitty, blurring all the images."

Jace asked, "Can you enlarge that one?"

The detective enlarged it is much as he could. But there was no way to tell.

"Did the coroner not bring it up?"

"The safety gear was three-quarters off as I recall." He

pulled out the notes. "The body was taken to the morgue, but the harnesses went back to the TxSAR crew. There was never a doubt from the beginning that this was a horrible accident. So no one went looking for evidence of foul play."

"And, therefore, no reason to keep the safety lines or harnesses." Jace studied the photos. "Why is it you don't have many photos? Because it wasn't a crime scene?"

"That's partly it. But we photograph all bodies we pull from the river. But we knew the cause in this case."

"You have any of Howard?"

The detective entered the name. "His body was recovered on the same day but not at the same time. I think it was about two or three hours afterward. He got caught up in some trees, a little bit farther up river."

"Here were photos of the body three-quarters immersed in the river. And another one on the bank. His harness and gear were intact, but there was no rope." The detective turned to look at Jace. "Is that what you're looking to see?"

"Any idea who accepted the gear?"

The detective shook his head. "Let me check and see if anything's in the notes." He went through several pages, then reached for his phone. "Hey, Parker. On those two drownings from the TxSAR group, any idea who collected the harnesses?"

He listened and wrote down a name. "Got it." He turned to Jace. "Troy did. I don't have a last name."

Jace nodded. "Okay. That confirms what Troy said. I was just checking." At that he stood to take his leave.

The detective shook their hands. "If you need anything, please let me know."

"Will do." Jace looked at Emily. "You want to add anything?"

She hunched her shoulders and glanced at him. "Should I?"

"You were fired for it, so he might as well know. If it's not important, the police will disregard it. But at least you've done your duty and made your firing worthwhile."

The detective asked, his voice puzzled, "You were fired over this?"

She took a deep breath, introduced herself and the company she'd worked for. "Because of Jace and Ice, I had been looking into the life insurance policies of these men who died."

The detective nodded. "Yes, we found those."

"Several other men at the same TxSAR Center have life insurance, and I wanted to make sure their policies had nothing to do with why these men were dying."

The detective sat back down and motioned for her to sit. "You found somebody else at the center with a life insurance policy?"

She nodded. "Peter."

Jace nodded. "I asked him about that."

Relief swept over her face. "Good. I wasn't allowed to give you his name." She sat back and looked at him. "Today I lost my job for nothing."

"Not necessarily," the detective said. "I understand you didn't get permission to share that name."

"No, and I wasn't allowed to give Ice any information either. I hadn't thought it was a big deal. Neither did Wilson. But the head office wasn't happy. Not to mention I told Jace about the earlier hacking incident. So my job was kind of on the line from that point forward." She groaned. "And of course Ice informed the police, things that I didn't have the authority to share with her," she said honestly.

The detective leaned forward. "What hacking incident?"

She glanced over at Jace again. "You're sure?"

"Oh, yeah, I'm sure."

She lunged into a tale about how the company had been hacked a few months before she started working for them.

"When we're looking at who had life insurance and whether these people were being killed for the payouts, we had to figure out how anybody would know," Jace said. "And that's when she mentioned the hacking."

"So the entire database was hacked for personal information about the policies' beneficiaries and policy owners," the detective recapped.

She sat back and shrugged.

"Well, that's interesting." He glanced at Jace. "Thank you for bringing her in."

"It might not be related," Jace said. "But we certainly didn't want to take a chance. We had to know who had life insurance policies."

"*If* it's even related to the killings," the detective added. "Sometimes I think about the perfect motive behind a murder, only to find out it was something so damn simple."

"And that's exactly what it might have been," Jace said. "But the working theory I have is so simple it's hardly worth killing over."

"Care to share that theory?" the detective asked.

Emily leaned forward. "Yes. What is it you're thinking about?"

"I wondered if it had something to do with the hierarchy within the TxSAR units."

"As to who got called out, who didn't? That type of thing?" she asked.

Jace exchanged a glance with the detective. "Possibly."

Then his phone rang. Jace pulled it out. "It's John. I left him a message earlier." He answered the phone and said, "Hi, John. What's up?"

"I was wondering if we could meet."

"Sure. Where and when? And what about?"

"I have this horribly nasty suspicion that I know what's going on. And I'd hate for that to be the case."

"You want to tell me now?"

"No. I'd rather do it in person. You can tell me if I'm being foolish or not. I don't want to sound foolish over the phone." He took a deep breath. "I feel pretty rattled."

"Are you in any danger?"

John took another deep breath. "I could be. I really could be. Yet it seems so foolish."

"Where are you?"

"I'm at home still."

"We'll be there in fifteen minutes," Jace said. "Don't go anywhere. Don't let anybody else in. Got it?"

"Got it."

Jace put away his phone and stood, grasping Emily's hand. "John wants to see me. He's afraid his own life is in danger. We're about fifteen minutes out."

"Do you want police backup?"

Jace shook his head. "But a ghost car on the block wouldn't be a bad idea," he said. "Or a plain clothes detective absolutely. But I don't want to put a police presence there in case the killer's watching."

The detective stood. "In that case I'm coming. I'll meet you on the same block. Give me the address."

Jace gave him the address, and the three of them walked out.

The detective said, "I'll park back a building or two. Before you enter, we need to meet and make sure everything's okay. I'm not having you walk into a situation that could already be ugly."

Jace nodded. "I can do that."

Emily leaned over and whispered to the detective, "He can do that. Jace does ugly."

Jace shook his head, gripped her hand, and tugged her toward his truck. "We'll be there in ten."

IN THE TRUCK she turned to him. "Can you tell me now?"

He shook his head. "No. Let's hear what John has to say."

She nodded. "Was it the right thing to tell the police?"

"Yes, it was. Particularly if it's related. Even if not related, it's still the right thing. The company had a responsibility to inform its clients about the fact that confidential information had been hacked. That they haven't done so is a serious breach of ethics."

"Yet I feel guilty," she announced.

"Get over it."

She laughed. "Is life that simple?"

"It so is. You made a decision. You know it was the right one. Now you have to adjust to the fallout."

"You act like you know what you're talking about. Was that what it was like for you when you left the military?"

He gave a clipped nod as he turned the truck to the left through an intersection. "Exactly. Just like that."

"Did it take you a year to adjust?"

He turned his gaze her way and gave her a crooked smile. "It did. But you're much better than I am. You can do it today."

At that she laughed. "Like hell."

"Okay. I see you'll need a few days," he said cheerfully.

She shook her head. "I don't even know if I want to stay in the same industry."

"Were you good at it?"

"I was very good at it," she said seriously. "It's also fairly depressing."

"You were helping people. Does it not make you feel good when you close a case?"

She sat quietly and thought about it. "If it's a clear-cut answer, yes. But, if I don't have a clear-cut answer, no."

"Any kind of job will have similar problems."

"I know all jobs have issues. None are perfect," she admitted. "When you can take a killer off the streets and put him in jail, then it's a great feeling. When I take somebody down who defrauded the insurance company, yet thinking it doesn't matter, I feel good to know they've been caught and the payment stopped. If it's much more severe, like a murder, then of course it's a great feeling. But so many slip through the cracks, and I know in some cases there are no right answers. I don't have access or any way to get the answers I need. And that's very frustrating. Sometimes I need a whole investigation and hire somebody, like Ice."

"Well, that's what we're here for. Most of the time we do security details and supersecret military cases or rescue kidnapped family members of high-profile clients."

"That's terrible," she said. "How did you end up with me?"

He chuckled. "I do not consider doing something to stop a killer targeting life insurance payouts as being at the bottom of the pile."

"And we have yet to prove anything in this is criminal."

He gave her a steely smile. "I suspect it will break itself

wide open today."

She gasped. "Really? Obviously Lyle's death was murder. And to me that's an entirely different story than Ronnie and Howard."

"One of the reasons Ice wanted the records was to make sure other TxSAR members who'd died with policies hadn't been murdered too."

"I hear that's where you've been heading mentally, but I don't understand why. What could possibly be the motive? These people were volunteers, out there helping the public. I mean, if this is somebody who shows up at all these natural disasters, why would he single out a TxSAR individual? Unless he was upset that one of his own loved ones wasn't saved? But even that doesn't make any sense."

"It never makes any sense until we get all the bits and pieces together," he said. "Even then there's no guarantee it will make perfect sense to you."

He pointed up ahead. "That's John's building. And there's the detective. Take a look around. See anyone around the apartment? He's in the first apartment on the bottom floor, left corner."

She turned her attention to the apartment. "I can't see anyone."

"Good."

"Are we taking the detective in with us?"

"Not at the beginning. I don't want anything to stop John from talking."

"That makes sense. There is something so very imposing about having a police officer there when you're tattling on someone."

"It's not tattling. You share the truth as you know it." He turned off the truck engine. "Sit here while I talk to the detective."

Chapter 14

J ACE HOPPED OUT of the vehicle and walked up to the detective's car. He bent down to the open window, and they spoke for a few minutes. She didn't have a clue what was going on. She could feel a sense of excitement. The tension in the air indicated they would finally get to the bottom of this.

When he returned to the truck, he walked directly to her side, opened the door, and held it for her. She slid out, and, with her arm in his, they walked toward the apartment.

"It took us a bit longer to get here than the fifteen minutes you said."

He nodded. "Hopefully he's still here. The traffic was brutal."

They knocked on the apartment door, and, when a woman's voice answered, Jace identified himself. She opened the door and let him and Emily in, then closed it. "You just missed him. He would stay and talk to you, but apparently there's been an accident near the center. One of the other crewmembers was involved, one he was close to, so he went running. Said he'd call you when he was back."

"Damn," Jace said in a soft voice. "Has he gone to the center itself?"

She nodded. "Yes."

Jace turned toward the door, then looked at John's wife.

"Who was the call from?"

"Amber."

"Thank you."

He strode to the truck so damn fast, Emily could barely keep up. He was already talking into his phone. "Meet us at the center."

"Did you call the detective?"

He nodded and pointed to the detective's car now heading out into the main traffic. "Get in," he barked. "We have to go to the center, and we have to go now."

"You want to tell me what's going on?"

"Another TxSAR member has been injured. Some kind of an incident close to the center. John's gone to help."

She sat quietly as he drove fast but not aggressively. Even now knowing time was important, he wasn't taking any chances.

"I hope nobody else dies," she said in a small voice.

"I'd be okay if one of them did."

Startled, she turned to look at him. "What?"

He glanced over at her. "Haven't you guessed by now?"

"Guessed what?"

"The person doing all the killing is one of the TxSAR team."

Emily gasped and sank into her seat. She could only stare at him wordlessly. In her mind all she could think of was how absolutely horrible that someone would do that.

THEY RACED INTO the center's parking lot. The detective was already out of his car. Together the three ran inside the main building. The front reception was empty. The office empty. Jace glanced around and bolted through the double doors toward the back. There he saw Amber. "Amber, where is John?"

Startled, she said, "He just left with Troy."

"Who was hurt?"

"Peter. The rocks slipped while they were practicing water rescues, and he's stuck between a couple big ones."

"What are you working on?" the detective asked. "I didn't hear any call for TxSAR or police backup."

Amber's face lit up in surprise. "No, it was a training mission. Peter fell, and his leg got pinned by two rocks. They've gone to help him." She looked at the three of them. "I'm heading out to the site now too. I believe paramedics have been called."

"We'll follow you," Jace said.

She nodded. "I'm bringing some of the gear for the guys."

Jace motioned to Emily. "Come on. Back to the truck."

Emily followed him. "I still don't understand what this is all about."

The detective got in his car, but this time Jace was in his truck and pulling out right behind Amber as she drove an SUV. He followed her onto the side roads that wound up and around the area. Ten minutes later she pulled onto the side shoulder and parked alongside several other vehicles. Jace pulled up behind her.

He glanced at Emily. "Make sure you stay as part of the crowd."

She frowned at him. "Why?"

He was already outside, racing around toward her. "I don't have time to explain. I need to know you're safe."

She shrugged. "No problem. I'll see what the others are up to."

He nodded, pointing to where the crowd was gathered. "Stay there." And he took off.

She walked to the crowd. Several people looked at her and frowned. She shrugged. "I came with Jace and the detective."

"Detective?"

She nodded but didn't explain. How could she? She didn't know anything.

A river was below, maybe twelve feet from where she stood, but the bank went on for a mile—or seemed to. It was slippery from the recent heavy rains. It didn't seem to slow Jace at all. He was already at the site where Peter sat with his leg pinned. She recognized several other men as being from the TxSAR team from their outfits. On man was ten to twelve feet into the river. Some of the men wore harnesses, and a couple more stood just inside the water, waiting to help.

Jace was not in any way geared up for this kind of activity. He didn't even have decent boots on for the unstable ground or the river. But she knew making any comment would be useless. Not only would he not hear her but, even if he could, he wouldn't listen. She saw the surprise on the others' faces as they saw him. The atmosphere was calm. There was no yelling or anger.

The pain on Peter's face was visible as she turned to look at Amber. "How did that happen?"

Amber shrugged. "When the rivers have a lot of force, the rocks become unstable. It doesn't take much to make them move."

"And you're the one who called John to come help Peter?"

"Yes. John's got experience with this kind of stuff. We

wanted to make sure Peter was rescued before there was any permanent damage to his leg."

At that Emily winced. "Right. That's not exactly something anybody wants."

Amber lowered her voice. "Troy has lots of experience but not as a leader."

Emily didn't know if it was her imagination, but she thought she heard a flat tone, as if Amber didn't like Troy. "Must be tough to see any of your friends get hurt."

"It's worse to see them dead." At that Amber turned and walked back to her SUV.

She had not seemed that upset, but this whole business was pretty damn upsetting.

Emily glanced at the rest of the group hanging around, but she didn't know anyone. With a bright smile she said, "You guys in the TxSAR training group?"

Several of them nodded. "We came for a training session. Then things went bad."

"You get some real experience in saving someone," she joked gently. Several laughed. She realized that, to them, it probably wasn't the best of days.

While she was trying to get information, her options were limited. She didn't think she would get too many answers here. She waited at the top as the men below clustered around pry bars used to shift rocks, and finally Peter was free. But he wasn't able to walk. With Jace and John working together, they created a seat with their entwined arms and carried Peter up the embankment. An ambulance arrived just then. They put him up on a stretcher and took off. The whole process took probably thirty to forty minutes, but it seemed to happen so fast with everyone busy doing something. She watched in fascination, having never seen a rescue like that before.

Suddenly Jace was beside her, dripping wet, a hard look on his face. Her heart sank as she looked at him. "Is that what you expected?"

He slanted a glance her way. "We got here in time to make sure it didn't happen again."

She gasped in understanding. "Really?"

He gave her a clipped nod. "Really."

"Do you have any proof?"

He shook his head. "No, I don't."

A man in charge told everyone to pack up and head back. That he'd proceed to the hospital to make sure the reports were filled out.

John walked over and shook Jace's hand. He smiled at Emily. "I didn't mean for you guys to come down here."

"We wanted to make sure there were no more deaths," Jace said.

John winced. "Maybe I was wrong about that."

Jace shook his head. "I doubt it. I really doubt it.

"You doubt what?" the leader asked with a belligerent tone to his voice. "How the hell do you keep popping up and getting in our faces?"

Emily frowned. "That's hardly fair," she stated, then read the name on the newcomer's jacket—Troy. "Jace came to help."

Troy glared at her. He shook his head. "Out, goddammit." He stormed off, but Jace called out, "I guess I upset your plans then?"

Troy spun around, shock on his face. "What are you talking about? I didn't have any plans here. We were training."

"Sure, that's a great way to get rid of somebody, isn't it?"

Troy spread his legs into a wider stance and placed his fist on his hips. "What the hell are you saying?"

"I'm saying, you meant for more than another accident here," Jace said, his gaze watchful.

Emily shook her head. She wished this wasn't happening here and now. But, behind Troy, she could see the detective leaning against Troy's truck, listening, and he wouldn't allow Troy to take off. She glanced at John who had gone incredibly still. As if watching a western shootout in progress.

"I'm saying you killed Ronnie and Howard this year and Ken Foster last year."

Troy's eyebrows shot up. "Now wait a minute. Those three men were all good, honorable men who died in accidents. Doing what they love to do. Which was rescuing and helping others."

If she hadn't been looking so closely, she wouldn't have seen it. But she did. That whisper of fear that crossed Troy's face. And she wondered and worried. *Please don't let something like that be the truth.* It would be too horrible to imagine Ronnie dying because of this man. Why would Troy do something like that?

"That's true. They were the best of men. But they died by your hand. The same as I'm pretty sure Peter's accident was one you engineered. It was the only way you could lure John to the scene. You knew he'd mentored Peter, and that, if Peter was in trouble, John would step up, regardless of his fear and pain and sense of loss."

"Of course he'd come to Peter's rescue. We all came to Peter's rescue," Troy said, his voice blustering and angry. He spread his arms open wide. "You did see the whole lot of us here, right?"

"And I did see you leading the charge to rescue." Jace

nodded.

"Right, like I always do. I've been volunteering here, been part of the center, for close to twenty years." He shook his head. "How dare you accuse me of doing something wrong. I've invested my entire life here, every free weekend. Anytime somebody needed me, I was there."

"And yet all those years you were never the leader of the center. Never the one they looked up to. You were never the manager, the organizer, the boss," Jace said, his voice forceful and yet quiet.

So much damn power was packed into that accusation that it was like a visceral punch to the other man's gut. She watched Troy take the blow, absorb it, and turn it into fury.

"And," Jace challenged, "the others preferred the leaders they had. Ken Foster was here for what, a decade? Until you arranged for him to have an *accident*," Jace said.

"Are you nuts?" Troy cried out. "Are you seriously implying I had something to do with those men's deaths?"

"I'm not implying any longer," Jace said. "Not only did you engineer the accidents but you murdered those men."

John sucked in his breath. The detective straightened. Yet the silence from the group was deafening for a moment.

Then Troy snorted. "And why would I do that?"

"Who is it that took over after Ken Foster was killed?"

"You know who took over. Ronnie did."

Jace turned to John and said, "How was Ronnie elected for the position?"

"By our votes. Troy was a contender but didn't have the same experience as Ronnie. Neither did Troy have the same respect from the team, and that makes a huge difference. Ronnie was the man who had all the experience and the respect."

"But Troy couldn't handle that. You didn't have all the experience, did you, Troy?"

"I had equal amounts of experience. We both had the same experience, a number of years of dedication, but he got the promotion," Troy spat out. "I should've gotten it."

And then it hit her. "Oh, my God, you killed him because he got the position you wanted. Then you killed his cousin because, as soon as Ronnie was dead, Howard would automatically step in to take his place because he was the next in line for the position."

She stared at the river, looked at John, and then at Troy. "You were afraid John would come back to the center, and the team would vote him in as the next leader. You couldn't allow that to happen." She shook her head and turned to Jace. "The life insurance was secondary."

"That's preposterous," Troy snapped. "Why would I do that?"

"Why wouldn't you?" Jace said. "After all, it wasn't a crime in your mind to kill these men, was it, Troy? You left their families with a hefty life insurance policy, didn't you? So by killing the men, you did everybody a favor. In your warped mind, the money made up for the deaths. Even though the wives suffered, they got one million bucks. No way for *you* to get that million dollars, but it helped you feel better about killing their spouses." Jace stared at Troy, seeing his face twist in anger. "You didn't have to kill these men. Yet you did. And you didn't give a damn because everybody got money, was better off with them gone, weren't they? It let you justify your actions." Jace shook his head. "But you were so wrong. These families wanted those men alive, with them for decades to come. They didn't want the damn money."

In a hard voice John added, "Is that why you suggested I get a life insurance policy after Ronnie died? So when my turn to die came around, my dearly beloved Mary wouldn't suffer more than she had to?"

Emily stared at Troy in shock. "That is so incredibly ugly."

"And how many others did you kill to further your own interests, to climb the social ladder, to get the position you thought you deserved?" Jace asked.

"It's not my fault," Troy roared. "If they'd given me a chance, I wouldn't have had to force them out."

"*Force them out?* You *killed* them."

"I did not! The river did that!" He made a motion with his hand to the water below. "I didn't hold their heads underwater. That was the river."

"Are you sure? Because we have a videotape of a third man with Ronnie and Howard at that vehicle. All clustered in the same place."

"And I told you that was the man they rescued." Troy shook his head at them. "You're making me out to be a bad guy here. I didn't do anything."

"But the man in the vehicle didn't have on a helmet. That third man was you. You went back into the river after you brought the truck over and got out the lines. While in the water, you made your way to Ronnie. But in all the confusion, you were counting on no one noticing who was where," Jace said, his tone glacial. "While there, you either held Ronnie underwater or slammed his head into something hard to knock him out. And Howard, busy trying to get the survivor to shore, didn't realize Ronnie was in trouble until Howard came back to see what was keeping his cousin at the vehicle. Then you gave Howard the exact same treatment as

Ronnie, didn't you? All that was left was to cut their lines and let the river have them."

Emily stared in horror as Troy's face worked, coming up with an excuse to justify what he'd done. How could he though? There was no excuse.

"How could you?" she cried out. "Ronnie was a decent man. So was Howard."

Troy looked at her. "Who the hell are you anyway?"

She stuck out her chin. "Ronnie's ex-wife, that's who. I knew the family. I knew both of them." She shook her head. "I worked at the insurance company where they had their policies."

"Easy," Jace whispered. He put a hand on her shoulder to calm her down. That's when she realized she'd taken several steps toward Troy, and her hands were clenched into fists. She was ready to attack Troy for what he'd done.

She stared at Troy. "You're a monster. You killed three men. God only knows how many others you planned on killing. John was today, wasn't he? Somehow John would have an accident out here while he was saving Peter."

At that Troy seemed to blow a gasket. "You don't know what the hell you're talking about. You don't know what it's like to be passed over time and time again. I gave my entire life to this organization. And they never gave me anything back."

"You don't volunteer like this to get something in re-turn," Emily cried out. "You do it to help people. That's the difference between you and Ronnie and Howard and Ken. They did it to help people. You did it to help yourself."

The detective stepped up behind Troy. Before he realized it, he had handcuffs on his wrists. Yet he kept spouting, "It's not fair. It's not fair. I couldn't even afford life insurance for myself. And yet not only did they do what they loved but they were well-loved for it. Now that they're gone, their families are all fine and dandy with the money. All I wanted was to run the center, to be looked up to, like they were."

"The other two men?" Emily asked. "Lyle and Richard? Did you kill them too?"

He snorted. "I wish I had. I should have, but they weren't worth the effort." He shook his head. "No, I didn't. And if I had, it wouldn't have been so obvious."

Sounds of sirens approached, and Emily realized the detective must've called for backup. She turned to Jace. "If he didn't kill them, who did?"

He glanced at her. "The methodologies said it wasn't Troy. Like he said, he would've made it less obvious. He would have used an accident scene, like he did for the three he did kill. He wouldn't have run over one, and he wouldn't have poured water down the throat of the other."

She stared at him in bewilderment. "Then who? Who killed them?"

He stared at her. "You might get your wish after all."

She gasped. "Sicily?" she shrieked. "You're serious?"

He nodded. "It's up to the police to prove it, but I'm pretty darn sure she and her current lover decided to kill her husband and ex-boyfriend for the insurance money. A convenient way to get rid of two problems and land a heavy-duty payday without working for it."

Emily was too flabbergasted to say anything. Her jaw dropped, and she stared at him. "I didn't really want her to have done it," she said when she could speak again. "But the woman obviously didn't give a damn about poor Lyle."

"No, it looks like she didn't."

He put an arm around her, turned to face John, and asked, "John, are you okay?"

Emily studied the man and realized how much he'd aged in the last few minutes.

He nodded. "I am now. There was something so futile about helping to rescue others only to lose our own men. Wondering if we were even doing anything to help protect our own people ..." He shook his head. "I know it sounds twisted and wrong, but I feel better knowing Troy murdered them, and it wasn't the men's lack of care or training or that the job itself was too big. I feel like I can come back to the center and handle it now. The others need me. Particularly after they find out what Troy's done."

The detective moved Troy to the cop car, but Troy shouted at them the whole way. She deliberately blocked out his insults.

Jace stepped between her and the sight of Troy being loaded into the vehicle. He tilted her chin up and said, "Don't even think about it."

The detective walked over and shook Jace's hand. "Now that was nicely done." He looked at Emily. "At least you know the three beneficiaries of these men's families weren't part of it."

She nodded. "But it is on the other two cases. Jace thinks it was Sicily Ranger Cowichan."

Detective Dickerson nodded. "I spoke to Jace about it earlier. We've picked up both her and her boyfriend for questioning. If it's them, we'll find out. One may turn on the other. A funnel was found inside the boyfriend's SUV. If we confirm any DNA from Richard Manton on the funnel, then we'll know exactly who had a hand in this."

"But why pour water down his throat?" Emily asked.

"To tie it to the deaths of the others. They didn't know the other three men had been murdered. This way they figured they could make the issue cloudy enough that nobody would know it was them. Water in the lungs can kill days later. Maybe they'd planned to drive Manton off the road into the river that evening, but his body was discovered too quickly. The coroner had the water analyzed. It was river water. So they had collected the water to pour into his lungs. Meaning it was premeditated. Lyle was killed by a blow to the head, then run over to make it look like a hit-and-run, which we've traced to the boyfriend's vehicle. Richard was likely killed beforehand, but the coroner can't place the time of death any closer. We are tracing the boyfriend's movements around that same time. Likely he knocked out Richard as he was getting into his car, the blows easy to confuse as ones from the fight with Lyle. Then simply shoved in the funnel and poured water in his lungs. Messy maybe but a ton of water wasn't involved."

She shook her head. "This is unbelievable."

"That's five good and caring men murdered?" John asked.

Jace nodded. "Two by the woman in question. One man was the woman's husband. The other was her ex-boyfriend. And then Troy killed three, at least three …" He turned to look at the detective. "I hope you'll take a good look at that issue before you close these cases."

The detective nodded. "We'll contact the insurance company to get a list of other payouts from other men in the TxSAR group. I suspect these were Troy's only victims, but we won't close the case until we check for sure." He turned to Emily. "Are you staying close by? We might need you to answer some questions."

She nodded. "You can always get me through my cell, but I have no idea where I'm going now that I've lost my job. And apparently the hacking wasn't even an issue."

"It's an issue," the detective said. "Don't you worry. We'll be broaching it with the company."

She nodded. "I can't say that staying here feels right at the moment. Honestly my skin's crawling with the idea of being in this town now. I'd like to get the hell away."

"You have Ice's phone number, and you have mine," Jace said. "You can get a hold of her through one of us anyway."

The two turned to John, and Jace asked, "Do you need a lift back?"

He shook his head and pointed to the truck Troy had driven. "I'll return this one to the center. It'll be a long time before we begin to recover from this."

"One of the best ways to recover," Emily said, "is to hold a memorial for the men who died at the hands of others. They were all preventable deaths, and they were all caused by ego or simple greed, one way or another. What a waste."

John nodded, shook Jace's hand, and said, "You two take care of yourselves." He turned, walked to the truck, hopped in, and, with a final wave, drove away.

"We wouldn't have known if you hadn't brought this to our attention. And," the detective said, "for that, Emily, we thank you." He then proceeded to his car.

As he drove away with Troy, Emily brightened. "That's right. I was worried something odd was going on here. It was partly my job and partly because I had such a connection to these men."

"Well, you were right. Something foul was going on. They were all murdered. But not by the same person."

She sighed. "At least that witch won't get two million dollars for her efforts."

Jace laughed and put an arm around her shoulders, hugging her. "So now that we're both free agents"—he leaned over and kissed her on the temple—"where do you want to go?"

"Definitely not to a lake or river," she said with a laugh. "How about back to my place for the bottle of wine I have hidden in the cupboard?"

"And the near future?"

"It's wide open. So, you know, tonight you might be able to persuade me one direction or another." She chuckled at the look on his face and his waggling eyebrows. "At least I'll have fun as you try."

He cuddled her in his arms and kissed her, a deep drugging kiss that gave her every reason to believe in their future together. She couldn't wait.

Epilogue

A S HE DROVE toward the property, Rory knew he should have outright said he wasn't interested to Jace and Tyson. Nothing about the look of the massive cement compound rising in the darkness before him could make him feel this was *his* place. Not even temporarily.

It wasn't the most welcoming sight he'd ever seen. Nothing like the family ranch.

Then was that important at this stage of his life?

Hell, yeah. Like the other men in his unit, he'd been lost this last year. Maybe more lost than they'd been. Michael had had his own place where he'd holed up, and Jace had come to the ranch to help out Rory's family. An act Rory much appreciated, considering he was keeping the family ranch afloat while his brother, who'd been hurt in a tractor accident, recovered.

Rory would have gone to the ranch sooner if he'd known he'd been needed. But, damn it, how was he supposed to know if no one said anything? He hadn't lived in Texas anymore, which was where the ranch was. He'd stuck to California, even after leaving the military. Mostly because he didn't know where else to go. But having a reason to come home made it seem less like an excuse and more like a purpose.

How could he tell them that he was lost and wanted to

return to his roots? That would bring up a mess of questions he had no intention of answering.

Thankfully his father had called and told him what happened. Rory had flown home immediately to help out until Dennis was back on his feet. Rory intended to be there for a few months but had ended up there almost nine. He'd enjoyed those months. And then it was time to go.

His brother was back on his feet. The ranch had the boss back, and Rory was an unpaid ranch hand, getting in the way and struggling to let go of the reins and handing control back to Dennis.

After one particular argument he realized the problem was him. This wasn't his place. He was always welcome to visit, but it wasn't his home.

He didn't have one.

And the sense of being lost returned in a vicious wave.

He turned off the engine and stepped out of his battered pickup truck. He tilted his beat-up cowboy hat back off his forehead and looked at the imposing structure. The longer he looked at it, the better he felt. It was massive, ugly, and cold-looking, but it had a timelessness to it. It was solid. It had been built to withstand the world, the elements, time, basically anything Mother Nature could throw at it. It no longer looked ugly as much as it looked immovable. There was a certain comfort in that.

But he had to remember it wasn't his home. Michael might have bought property bordering it, but that was Michael. Not Rory. Michael had put down roots.

Rory was afraid he didn't have any to put down.

A nearby door opened suddenly, and he could see shadows as several people walked out. A security lamp turned on, highlighting the men standing in front of him.

Jace, Tyson, Michael. Easy men to identify. So many more stood beside them. And women …

Suddenly shy, he tilted his hand and, in a husky drawl, said, "Good evening."

"About time you got here," Jace said, stepping forward to slap him on the shoulder. "I was hoping you'd make it. How's Dennis doing?"

"He's back on top, so I figured maybe you guys could use a hand." Rory stepped forward, only now seeing Ice and Levi.

Ice's face lit up. "Rory?"

She raced toward him and threw her arms around him. "I'm so happy to see you. Levi told me that he'd offered you a job but hadn't said you'd answered."

"I didn't. I just arrived," he apologized and stepped back. Ice had adopted him into her friend group a long time ago. He studied her face. "This suits you."

She beamed. "It does indeed." But her gaze was intense, searching, and she wouldn't let him back away. Ever since she'd heloed in and picked him up, badly injured from a mission that had gone wrong, she'd kept an eye on him. She'd dragged him out with her friends time and time again for a few beers.

Levi stepped forward and shook Rory's hand with a grin on his face. "About time you got here."

And some of Rory's initial uneasiness dropped away.

Ice turned to look at Levi. "You didn't tell me that he was coming."

"I didn't know when he'd get here. I just let him know the door was always open. I figured he'd find his way eventually."

Ice's smile was so damn beautiful as she stared at Levi

that Rory suddenly wished someone was in his life who looked at him the same way. But he needed to get his own shit together first.

Levi swung his arm toward the doorway. "You've got a lot of friends here. Welcome home."

The wording stopped Rory for a long moment. Did Levi realize that was exactly what Rory was missing? A sense of home. And someone in it to share his life with.

Then a series of odd yips filled the air. He glanced down to see a fat puppy barely walking with several siblings behind it, all waddling toward them.

"Sorry," a tall brunette woman said. "They've had their bottle and now need to go to the bathroom, so I brought them outside. I didn't realize you were all out here."

"No problem. Louise, come meet Rory, the newest member of the team," Ice said.

Rory squatted down as one of the puppies struggled to make it to him, his nose quickly pushing into Rory's hand. He chuckled and scooped the pudge up. "What's this guy's name?"

"We're trying to come up with some," Levi said. "These guys are from Anna and Flynn's place. The mother has no milk, and Anna needed help feeding them, so we're fostering them until Anna can find homes."

Louise laughed. "Good luck with that." She smiled at Rory and reached out to shake his hand. "I'm a vet. I came to check out these little guys." She walked to her car as she said, "I can see they are all well looked after. I'll come back in a few days."

Rory, his arms full of adorableness, watched her drive away. When he turned to the others, he found a speculative look on Ice's face. He raised an eyebrow. "What's the matter?"

Jace snorted and said, "Don't worry about it. Give in now. It'll happen no matter what you do, so surrender to it from the start. It's easier that way."

Rory stared at him in confusion.

Levi grinned. "Come on inside. Looks like you'll fit right in."

This concludes Book 12 of Heroes for Hire: Jace's Jewel.

Read about Rory's Rose: Heroes for Hire, Book 13

Heroes for Hire: Rory's Rose (Book #13)

Rory is an animal lover. In his mind, any veterinarian who does as much pro bono work as Louise, the local vet, deserves his help when she gets into trouble…

Louise works long hours at her own veterinarian clinic. When she receives an unexpected delivery one day, complete with a dead deliveryman, a domino-series of events puts her and her clinic full of precious animals in danger.

Rory is the first to volunteer to keep her safe. Professional reasons quickly become personal. Louise is everything he's ever wanted and never expected to find in a single woman. He's looking forward to a future together, and the only way to ensure that is to stop whatever's endangering her and her animals.

Unfortunately, the killer isn't leaving a witness to his crimes. At first, Rory and the team at Legendary Securities make headway in discovering what's going on, but the tables turn in an instant and, for the first time since he joined the team, Rory's vision of a satisfactory resolution—and happily-ever-after—may not be in the cards.

Book 13 is available now!

To find out more visit Dale Mayer's website.

https://geni.us/DMRoryUniversal

Other Military Series by Dale Mayer

SEALs of Honor

Heroes for Hire

SEALs of Steel

The K9 Files

The Mavericks

Bullards Battle

Hathaway House

Terkel's Team

Ryland's Reach: Bullard's Battle
(Book #1)

Welcome to a new stand-alone but interconnected series from Dale Mayer. This is Bullard's story—and that of his team's. All raw, rough, incredibly capable men who have one goal: to find out who was behind the attack on their leader, before the attacker, or attackers, return to finish the job.

Stay tuned for more nonstop action as the men narrow down their suspects … and find a way to let love back into their own empty lives.

His rescue from the ocean after a horrible plane explosion was his top priority, in any way, shape, or form. A small sailboat and a nurse to do the job was more than Ryland hoped for.

When Tabi somehow drags him and his buddy Garret onboard and surprisingly gets them to a naval ship close by, Ryland figures he'd used up all his luck and his friend's too. Sure enough, those who attacked the plane they were in weren't content to let him slowly die in the ocean. No. Surviving had made him a target all over again.

Tabi isn't expecting her sailing holiday to include the rescue of two badly injured men and then to end with the loss of her beloved sailboat. Her instincts save them, but now she finds it tough to let them go—even as more of Bullard's team members come to them—until it becomes apparent that not only are Bullard and his men still targets ... but she is too.

B ULLARD CHECKED THAT the helicopter was loaded with their bags and that his men were ready to leave.

He walked back one more time, his gaze on Ice. She'd never looked happier, never looked more perfect. His heart ached, but he knew she remained a caring friend and always would be. He opened his arms; she ran into them, and he held her close, whispering, "The offer still stands."

She leaned back and smiled up at him. "Maybe if and when Levi's been gone for a long enough time for me to forget," she said in all seriousness.

"That's not happening. You two, now three, will live long and happy lives together," he said, smiling down at the woman knew to be the most beautiful, inside and out. She would never be his, but he always kept a little corner of his heart open and available, in case she wanted to surprise him and to slide inside.

And then he realized she'd already been a part of his heart all this time. That was a good ten to fifteen years by now. But she kept herself in the friend category, and he understood because she and Levi, partners and now parents, were perfect together.

Bullard reached out and shook Levi's hand. "It was a hell of a blast," he said. "When you guys do a big splash, you really do a *big* splash."

Ice laughed. "A few days at home sounds perfect for me now."

"It looks great," he said, his hands on his hips as he surveyed the people in the massive pool surrounded by the palm trees, all designed and decked out by Ice. Right beside all the war machines that he heartily approved of. He grinned at her. "When are you coming over to visit?" His gaze went to Levi, raising his eyebrows back at her. "You guys should come over for a week or two or three."

"It's not a bad idea," Levi said. "We could use a long holiday, just not yet."

"That sounds familiar." Bullard grinned. "Anyway, I'm off. We'll hit the airport and then pick up the plane and head home." He added, "As always, call if you need me."

Everybody raised a hand as he returned to the helicopter and his buddy who was flying him to the airport. Ice had volunteered to shuttle him there, but he hadn't wanted to take her away from her family or to prolong the goodbye. He hopped inside, waving at everybody as the helicopter lifted. Two of his men, Ryland and Garret, were in the back seats. They always traveled with him.

Bullard would pick up the rest of his men in Australia. He stared down at the compound as he flew overhead. He preferred his compound at home, but damn they'd done a nice job here.

With everybody on the ground screaming goodbye, Bullard sailed over Houston, heading toward the airport. His two men never said a word. They all knew how he felt about Ice. But not one of them would cross that line and say anything. At least not if they expected to still have jobs.

It was one thing to fall in love with another man's woman, but another thing to fall in love with a woman who was so unique, so different, and so absolutely perfect that you knew, just knew, there was no hope of finding anybody else like her. But she and Levi had been together way before Bullard had ever met her, which made it that much more heartbreaking.

Still, he'd turned and looked forward. He had a full roster of jobs himself to focus on when he got home. Part of him was tired of the life; another part of him couldn't wait to head out on the next adventure. He managed to run everything from his command centers in one or two of his locations. He'd spent a lot of time and effort at the second one and kept a full team at both locations, yet preferred to spend most of his time at the old one. It felt more like home to him, and he'd like to be there now, but still had many more days before that could happen.

The helicopter lowered to the tarmac, he stepped out, said his goodbyes and walked across to where his private plane waited. It was one of the things that he loved, being a pilot of both helicopters and airplanes, and owning both birds himself.

That again was another way he and Ice were part of the same team, of the same mind-set. He'd been looking for another woman like Ice for himself, but no such luck. Sure, lots were around for short-term relationships, but most of them couldn't handle his lifestyle or the violence of the world that he lived in. He understood that.

The ones who did had a hard edge to them that he found difficult to live with. Bullard appreciated everybody's being alert and aware, but if there wasn't some softness in the women, they seemed to turn cold all the way through.

As he boarded his small plane, Ryland and Garret following behind, Bullard called out in his loud voice, "Let's go, slow pokes. We've got a long flight ahead of us."

The men grinned, confident Bullard was teasing, as was his usual routine during their off-hours.

"Well, we're ready, not sure about you though …" Ryland said, smirking.

"We're waiting on you this time," Garret added with a chuckle. "Good thing you're the boss."

Bullard grinned at his two right-hand men. "Isn't that the truth?" He dropped his bags at one of the guys' feet and said, "Stow all this stuff, will you? I want to get our flight path cleared and get the hell out of here."

They'd all enjoyed the break. He tried to get over once a year to visit Ice and Levi and same in reverse. But it was time to get back to business. He started up the engines, got confirmation from the tower. They were heading to Australia for this next job. He really wanted to go straight back to Africa, but it would be a while yet. They'd refuel in Honolulu.

Ryland came in and sat down in the copilot's spot, buckled in, then asked, "You ready?"

Bullard laughed. "When have you ever known me *not* to be ready?" At that, he taxied down the runway. Before long he was up in the air, at cruising level, and heading to Hawaii. "Gotta love these views from up here," Bullard said. "This place is magical."

"It is once you get up above all the smog," he said. "Why Australia again?"

"Remember how we were supposed to check out that newest compound in Australia that I've had my eye on? Besides the alpha team is coming off that ugly job in Sydney. We'll give them a day or two of R&R then head home."

"Right. We could have some equally ugly payback on that job."

Bullard shrugged. "That goes for most of our jobs. It's the life."

"And don't you have enough compounds to look after?"

"Yes I do, but that kid in me still looks to take over the world. Just remember that."

"Better you go home to Africa and look after your first two compounds," Ryland said.

"Maybe," Bullard admitted. "But it seems hard to not continue expanding."

"You need a partner," Ryland said abruptly. "That might ease the savage beast inside. Keep you home more."

"Well, the only one I like," he said, "is married to my best friend."

"I'm sorry about that," Ryland said quietly. "What a shit deal."

"No," Bullard said. "I came on the scene last. They were always meant to be together. Especially now they are a family."

"If you say so," Ryland said.

Bullard nodded. "Damn right, I say so."

And that set the tone for the next many hours. They landed in Hawaii, and while they fueled up everybody got off to stretch their legs by walking around outside a bit as this was a small private airstrip, not exactly full of hangars and tourists. Then they hopped back on board again for takeoff.

"I can fly," Ryland offered as they took off.

"We'll switch in a bit," Bullard said. "Surprisingly, I'm doing okay yet, but I'll let you take her down."

"Yeah, it's still a long flight," Ryland said studying the islands below. It was a stunning view of the area.

"I love the islands here. Sometimes I just wonder about the benefit of, you know, crashing into the sea, coming up on a deserted island, and finding the simple life again," Bullard said with a laugh.

"I hear you," Ryland said. "Every once in a while, I wonder the same."

Several hours later Ryland looked up and said abruptly, "We've made good time considering we've already passed Fiji."

Bullard yawned.

"Let's switch."

Bullard smiled, nodded, and said, "Fine. I'll hand it over to you."

Just then a funny noise came from the engine on the right side.

They looked at each other, and Ryland said, "Uh-oh. That's not good news."

Boom!

And the plane exploded.

Find Bullard's Battle (Book #1) here!

To find out more visit Dale Mayer's website.

https://geni.us/DMRylandUniversal

Damon's Deal: Terkel's Team (Book #1)

Welcome to a brand-new connected series of intrigue, betrayal, and … murder, from the *USA Today* best-selling author Dale Mayer. A series with all the elements you've come to love, plus so much more… including psychics!

A betrayal from within has Terkel frantic to protect those he can, as his team falls one by one, from a murderous killer he helped create.

ICE POURED HERSELF a coffee and sat down at the compound's massive dining room table with the others. When her phone rang, she smiled at the number displayed. "Hey, Terk. How're you doing?" She put the call on Speakerphone.

"I'm okay," Terkel said, his voice distracted and tight.

"Terk?" Merk called from across the table. He got up and walked closer and sat across from Levi. "You don't sound too good, brother. What's up?"

"I'm fine," Terk said. "Or I will be. Right now, things are blown to shit."

"As in literally?" Merk asked.

"The entire group," Terk said, "they're all gone. I had a solid team of eight, and they're all gone."

"Dead?"

Several others stood to join them, gathered around Ice's phone. Levi stepped forward, his hand on Ice's shoulder. "Terk? Are they all dead?"

"No." Terk took a deep breath. "I'm not making sense. I'm sorry."

"Take it easy," Ice said, her voice calm and reassuring. "What do you mean, *they're all gone?*"

"All their abilities are gone," he said. "Something's happened to them. Somebody has deliberately removed whatever super senses they could utilize—or what we have been utilizing for the last ten years for the government." His tone was bitter. "When the US gov recently closed us down, they promised that our black ops department would never rise again, but I didn't expect them to attack us personally."

"What are you talking about?" Merk said in alarm, standing up now to stare at Ice's phone. "Are you in danger?"

"Maybe? I don't know," Terk said. "I need to find out exactly what the hell's going on."

"What can we do to help?" Ice asked.

Terk gave a broken laugh. "That's not why I'm calling. Well, it is, but it isn't."

Ice looked at Merk, who frowned, as he shook his head. Ice knew he and the others had heard Terk's stressed out tone and the completely confusing bits and pieces coming from his mouth. Ice said, "Terk, you're not making sense again. Take a breath and explain. Please. You're scaring me."

Terk took a long slow deep breath. "Tell Stone to open the gate," he said. "She's out there."

"Who's out there?" Levi asked, hopped up, looked outside, and shrugged.

"She's coming up the road now. You have to let her in."

"Who? Why?"

"*Because*," he said, "she's also harnessed with C-4."

"Jesus," Levi said, bolting to display the camera feeds to the big screen in the room. "Is it live?"

"It is, and she's been sent to you."

"Well, that's an interesting move," Ice said, her voice sharp, activating her comm to connect to Stone in the control room. "Who's after us?"

"I think it's rebels within the Iranian government. But it could be our own government. I don't know anymore," Terk snapped. "I also don't know how they got her so close to you. Or how they pinned your connection to me," he said. "I've been very careful."

"We can look after ourselves," Ice said immediately. "But who is this woman to you?"

"She's pregnant," he said, "so that adds to the intensity here."

"Understood. So who is the father? Is he connected somehow?"

There was silence on the other end.

Merk said, "Terk, talk to us."

"She's carrying my baby," Terk replied, his voice heavy.

Merk, his expression grim, looked at Ice, her face mirroring his shock. He asked, "How do you know her, Terk?"

"Brother, you don't understand," Terk said. "I've never met this woman before in my life." And, with that, the phone went dead.

Find Terkel's Team (Book #1) here!

To find out more visit Dale Mayer's website.

https://geni.us/DMTTDamonUniversal

Author's Note

Thank you for reading Jace's Jewel: Heroes for Hire, Book 12! If you enjoyed the book, please take a moment and leave a short review.

Dear reader,

I love to hear from readers, and you can contact me at my website: www.dalemayer.com or at my Facebook author page. To be informed of new releases and special offers, sign up for my newsletter or follow me on BookBub. And if you are interested in joining Dale Mayer's Reader Group, here is the Facebook sign up page.
http://geni.us/DaleMayerFBGroup

Cheers,
Dale Mayer

About the Author

Dale Mayer is a *USA Today* best-selling author, best known for her SEALs military romances, her Psychic Visions series, and her Lovely Lethal Garden cozy series. Her contemporary romances are raw and full of passion and emotion (Broken But … Mending, Hathaway House series). Her thrillers will keep you guessing (Kate Morgan, By Death series), and her romantic comedies will keep you giggling (*It's a Dog's Life*, a stand-alone novella; and the Broken Protocols series, starring Charming Marvin, the cat).

Dale honors the stories that come to her—and some of them are crazy, break all the rules and cross multiple genres!

To go with her fiction, she also writes nonfiction in many different fields, with books available on résumé writing, companion gardening, and the US mortgage system. All her books are available in print and ebook format.

Connect with Dale Mayer Online

Dale's Website – www.dalemayer.com
Twitter – @DaleMayer
Facebook Page – geni.us/DaleMayerFBFanPage
Facebook Group – geni.us/DaleMayerFBGroup
BookBub – geni.us/DaleMayerBookbub
Instagram – geni.us/DaleMayerInstagram
Goodreads – geni.us/DaleMayerGoodreads
Newsletter – geni.us/DaleNews

Also by Dale Mayer

Published Adult Books:

Bullard's Battle

Ryland's Reach, Book 1

Cain's Cross, Book 2

Eton's Escape, Book 3

Garret's Gambit, Book 4

Kano's Keep, Book 5

Fallon's Flaw, Book 6

Quinn's Quest, Book 7

Bullard's Beauty, Book 8

Bullard's Best, Book 9

Terkel's Team

Damon's Deal, Book 1

Kate Morgan

Simon Says… Hide, Book 1

Hathaway House

Aaron, Book 1

Brock, Book 2

Cole, Book 3

Denton, Book 4

Elliot, Book 5

Finn, Book 6

Gregory, Book 7

Heath, Book 8

Iain, Book 9

Jaden, Book 10

Keith, Book 11

Lance, Book 12

Melissa, Book 13

Nash, Book 14

Owen, Book 15

Hathaway House, Books 1–3

Hathaway House, Books 4–6

Hathaway House, Books 7–9

The K9 Files

Ethan, Book 1

Pierce, Book 2

Zane, Book 3

Blaze, Book 4

Lucas, Book 5

Parker, Book 6

Carter, Book 7

Weston, Book 8

Greyson, Book 9

Rowan, Book 10

Caleb, Book 11

Kurt, Book 12

Tucker, Book 13

Harley, Book 14

The K9 Files, Books 1–2

The K9 Files, Books 3–4

The K9 Files, Books 5–6

The K9 Files, Books 7–8

The K9 Files, Books 9–10

The K9 Files, Books 11–12

Lovely Lethal Gardens

Arsenic in the Azaleas, Book 1

Bones in the Begonias, Book 2

Corpse in the Carnations, Book 3

Daggers in the Dahlias, Book 4

Evidence in the Echinacea, Book 5

Footprints in the Ferns, Book 6

Gun in the Gardenias, Book 7

Handcuffs in the Heather, Book 8

Ice Pick in the Ivy, Book 9

Jewels in the Juniper, Book 10

Killer in the Kiwis, Book 11

Lifeless in the Lilies, Book 12

Murder in the Marigolds, Book 13

Lovely Lethal Gardens, Books 1–2

Lovely Lethal Gardens, Books 3–4

Lovely Lethal Gardens, Books 5–6

Lovely Lethal Gardens, Books 7–8

Lovely Lethal Gardens, Books 9–10

Psychic Vision Series

Tuesday's Child

Hide 'n Go Seek

Maddy's Floor

Garden of Sorrow

Knock Knock…

Rare Find

Eyes to the Soul

Now You See Her

Shattered

Into the Abyss

Seeds of Malice

Eye of the Falcon

Itsy-Bitsy Spider

Unmasked

Deep Beneath

From the Ashes

Stroke of Death

Ice Maiden

Snap, Crackle…

Psychic Visions Books 1–3

Psychic Visions Books 4–6

Psychic Visions Books 7–9

By Death Series

Touched by Death

Haunted by Death

Chilled by Death

By Death Books 1–3

Broken Protocols – Romantic Comedy Series

Cat's Meow

Cat's Pajamas

Cat's Cradle

Cat's Claus

Broken Protocols 1-4

Broken and… Mending

Skin

Scars

Scales (of Justice)

Broken but… Mending 1-3

Glory

Genesis

Tori

Celeste

Glory Trilogy

Biker Blues

Morgan: Biker Blues, Volume 1

Cash: Biker Blues, Volume 2

SEALs of Honor

Mason: SEALs of Honor, Book 1

Hawk: SEALs of Honor, Book 2

Dane: SEALs of Honor, Book 3

Swede: SEALs of Honor, Book 4

Shadow: SEALs of Honor, Book 5

Cooper: SEALs of Honor, Book 6

Heroes for Hire

Heroes for Hire, Books 10–12

Heroes for Hire, Books 13–15

SEALs of Steel

Badger: SEALs of Steel, Book 1

Erick: SEALs of Steel, Book 2

Cade: SEALs of Steel, Book 3

Talon: SEALs of Steel, Book 4

Laszlo: SEALs of Steel, Book 5

Geir: SEALs of Steel, Book 6

Jager: SEALs of Steel, Book 7

The Final Reveal: SEALs of Steel, Book 8

SEALs of Steel, Books 1–4

SEALs of Steel, Books 5–8

SEALs of Steel, Books 1–8

The Mavericks

Kerrick, Book 1

Griffin, Book 2

Jax, Book 3

Beau, Book 4

Asher, Book 5

Ryker, Book 6

Miles, Book 7

Nico, Book 8

Keane, Book 9

Lennox, Book 10

Gavin, Book 11

Shane, Book 12

Diesel, Book 13

Jerricho, Book 14

The Mavericks, Books 1–2

The Mavericks, Books 3–4

The Mavericks, Books 5–6

The Mavericks, Books 7–8

The Mavericks, Books 9–10

The Mavericks, Books 11–12

Collections

Dare to Be You…

Dare to Love…

Dare to be Strong…

RomanceX3

Standalone Novellas

It's a Dog's Life

Riana's Revenge

Second Chances

Published Young Adult Books:

Family Blood Ties Series

Vampire in Denial

Vampire in Distress

Vampire in Design

Vampire in Deceit

Vampire in Defiance

Vampire in Conflict

Vampire in Chaos

Vampire in Crisis

Vampire in Control

Vampire in Charge

Family Blood Ties Set 1–3

Family Blood Ties Set 1–5

Family Blood Ties Set 4–6

Family Blood Ties Set 7–9

Sian's Solution, A Family Blood Ties Series Prequel Novelette

Design series

Dangerous Designs

Deadly Designs

Darkest Designs

Design Series Trilogy

Standalone

In Cassie's Corner

Gem Stone (a Gemma Stone Mystery)

Time Thieves

Published Non-Fiction Books:

Career Essentials

Career Essentials: The Résumé

Career Essentials: The Cover Letter

Career Essentials: The Interview

Career Essentials: 3 in 1